"I felt like I was on a high-octane ride while reading." *5 stars, Amazon Review*

"These two characters are layered with irresistible traits and emotions that make them come alive on the page." *5 stars, GoodReads Review*

ALSO BY ANNA CAMPBELL

Claiming the Courtesan

Untouched

Tempt the Devil

Captive of Sin

My Reckless Surrender

Midnight's Wild Passion

The Sons of Sin Series:

Seven Nights in a Rogue's Bed

Days of Rakes and Roses

A Rake's Midnight Kiss

What a Duke Dares

A Scoundrel by Moonlight

Three Proposals and a Scandal

The Dashing Widows Series:

The Seduction of Lord Stone

Tempting Mr. Townsend

"This book is the reason Anna Campbell is a one-click author for me! Her characters are both likeable and charming. Her words seep into you, giving you a hot rush of joy that makes you yearn for the HEA! A must-read for all romantics!" *5 stars, GoodReads Review*

"The dynamic between Brock and the widowed Selina is hot, and their interactions are beautiful - a slow unfurling of discovering the other half of one's soul while the sexual tension ramps up so high it melts the snow. Delicious and tender by turn, this is a lovely story of two lost people finding one another." *Susanne Bellamy, bestselling author*

"Ms. Campbell has outdone herself with this book, absolutely a fantastic hot read, with an intriguing story." *5 stars, Goodreads Review*

"Ms. Campbell has written another simply divine love story." *5 stars, Amazon Review*

"A love story that will bring tears to your eyes and a smile to your lips. Do not miss this one!!" *5 stars, The Reading Wench*

"So luscious. So heartrending but so triumphant an ending, all in a novella length. I'll be rereading this one. Highly recommended to Campbell's fans." *5 stars, Amazon Review*

"This is a steamy historical romance that indulges all things lustful and pleasurable. Escapism at its best. This book ticks a lot of boxes. One of my favorites." *5 stars, GoodReads Review*

Winning Lord West

Pursuing Lord Pascal

Charming Sir Charles

Catching Captain Nash

Lord Garson's Bride

The Lairds Most Likely Series:

The Laird's Willful Lass

The Laird's Christmas Kiss

The Highlander's Lost Lady

The Highlander's Defiant Captive

The Highlander's Christmas Quest

The Highlander's English Bride

The Highlander's Forbidden Mistress

The Highlander's Christmas Countess

The Highlander's Rescued Maiden

The Highlander's Christmas Lassie

A Scandal in Mayfair Series:

One Wicked Wish

Two Secret Sins

Three Times Tempted

Christmas Stories:

The Winter Wife

Her Christmas Earl

A Pirate for Christmas

Mistletoe and the Major

A Match Made in Mistletoe

The Christmas Stranger

His Christmas Cinderella (in the anthology A Grosvenor Square Christmas)

Other Books:

These Haunted Hearts

Stranded with the Scottish Earl

The Highlander's Forbidden Mistress

The Lairds Most Likely Book 7

ANNA CAMPBELL

To my dear friend Vanessa Barneveld

CHAPTER ONE

Derwent Hall, Essex, December 1823

"You will arrive at Mowbray Place on Christmas Eve, and not too late either. Mamma likes her dinner at five o'clock on the dot."

Selina Martin struggled not to wince at her fiancé's hectoring tone. Was it her imagination that the walls of Derwent Hall's library with their Etruscan decorations closed in on her? Whether they did or not, she felt suffocated. "Yes, Cecil."

She and Cecil Canley-Smythe had been guests at this luxurious manor in Essex all week, while Cecil and Lord Derwent discussed business matters. But the visit had not proven a success. The other guests had been a disreputable selection, however blue their blood, and Cecil hadn't approved of the way they'd carried on with one another. Nor had the disreputable gathering approved of Cecil, with his propensity for laying down the law, even while in someone else's house. Tonight at dinner when Cecil announced that he and his betrothed were leaving in the morning, Selina had noted a general air of relief.

"You will also speak to the boy about restraining any excessive high spirits over the Festive Season. Mamma cannot abide undue noise."

"The boy" was her nine-year-old son, Gerald. Sometimes she doubted whether Cecil even remembered Gerald's name. A problem when he was about to become Gerald's stepfather.

Selina told herself that she could bear this. She could bear anything for her son's sake. "Yes, Cecil."

"And I hope you're not doing anything silly with your wedding dress. Mamma expects the ceremony to proceed with suitable dignity. You're a widow, and I'm a respectable man of mature years. Any unseemly frivolity won't reflect well on a person of my standing."

Mature years? He had that right. Despite how tightly he was tied to his mother's apron strings, he was fifty-five. Selina was only twenty-seven, even if right now she might feel like she was a hundred and seven.

Curling her fingers at her sides until her nails bit into her palms, she kept her voice calm. "I've chosen a plain cream frock without a train, Cecil. Nobody will accuse me of extravagance or vanity."

Selina hadn't selected her modest gown entirely because of Cecil's dislike for frivolity. Even purchasing such a simple dress had stretched her meager financial resources.

"I'm pleased to hear it. Now after I leave tomorrow, I'll be busy every day with my mills in Northumberland. Don't look for any letters. I won't have time to write to you."

"I understand. I won't trouble you either, unless something urgent comes up."

"Urgent?" He frowned in displeasure. "I'm not expecting anything urgent."

Well, the bride might yet jump off Westminster Bridge to avoid her nuptials, but that probably wouldn't count as urgent in Cecil's estimation. Whereas if Selina sewed a scrap of lace onto her wedding gown, he was sure to class that as an emergency.

"I can't imagine anything untoward will turn up," she said, with the meekness she'd learned to use during her first marriage to soothe her husband's erratic temper.

A log popped in the hearth, making her glance past her hulking fiancé with his wet lips and balding head to where a long, high-backed settle faced the fire. The imposing piece of furniture with its solid mahogany back dominated the room.

"See that there isn't." Cecil regarded her with a disapproval that she was sure she didn't deserve. "Mamma has always been worried that your youth makes you unreliable. I told her that you're a sensible woman, and that marriage to a rich man won't turn your head. Don't make me a liar."

Selina wanted to tell Cecil's mamma to button her wrinkled lip, but defiance served no purpose. She chose this path with her eyes wide open. A show of spirit now would only toss her back to the wolves. Her and her son. "You can rely on me, Cecil."

His manner softened, and he gave her a smile. "I know I can, my dear. That's why I asked you to be my bride."

He no longer sounded like a sergeant dressing down a tardy recruit, but somehow that was worse than a scolding. The "my dear" made her hide a shudder. Because while Cecil was determined that in public she behaved like a sober widow, she suspected his private intentions weren't nearly so circumspect.

He wanted her in his bed. She'd known it from the first.

Lucky her.

"I'll make you a good wife."

"If I had the slightest doubt, I'd never have proposed. The world has always praised your devoted care of your late husband, despite his unfortunate wildness, and your comportment in widowhood has been exemplary." He stepped closer. "Now it grows late, and we both have a long journey in the morning."

While Cecil headed north, she returned to her humble lodgings in Marylebone to wait out the fortnight before the wedding on Boxing Day. The second week of that period at least offered Gerald's company, once his school closed for Christmas. But while she loved her son, she wasn't entirely looking forward to that either. Gerald had only met Cecil once, and he hadn't liked him. He wouldn't be slow to make his resentment of his future stepfather felt.

He was too young to understand why his mother gave herself into Cecil's keeping, and she'd done her best to hide how desperate things were in the Martin household. Selina had so many doubts about her forthcoming marriage, but the tragic truth was that if she didn't marry Cecil, she might end up on the streets. And if she did, she'd lose Gerald.

So she raised her chin and summoned a smile and battled to ignore how her stomach knotted with revulsion when Cecil kissed her cheek. In their eight weeks of betrothal, he'd never kissed her on the lips. But the reprieve was only temporary. She had no illusions that he'd keep his distance, once his ring was on her finger.

Damp lips skimmed her skin, and the overpowering scent of *Pomade de Nerole* made her dizzy. He stepped back before she could gag, thank heavens. "Shall I escort you to the staircase?"

She shook her head. "Thank you, but I need to choose a book, or I'll never sleep. You go ahead, and I'll see you in a fortnight."

Cecil was leaving early, so they wouldn't meet in the morning. The prospect of two weeks of freedom both exhilarated and troubled her. Fourteen days without her fiancé shouldn't feel like she dodged a death sentence. She had to reconcile herself to this marriage, or the years ahead would be too wretched to contemplate.

"Very well. It's not long now. I know the waiting grows wearisome, but you'll soon be my wife."

"Yes, Cecil." She hoped he didn't hear the dullness in her tone.

The heady sensation of freedom had lasted a mere second. Now she was back to sitting inside the condemned woman's cell, waiting for sentence to be carried out.

Once Cecil left, she moved across to one of the bookcases. Cecil liked women to read improving sermons, full of strictures on obedience and modesty. A spirit of rebellion had her pulling *Tom Jones* from the shelf.

"That was a remarkable demonstration of unbridled passion, if I ever heard one. When I listened to the two of you making such wanton promises to each other, you put me to the blush. My word, you did."

Oh, no. The deep sardonic drawl made Selina drop the book and whirl around with a horrified gasp. Cold hands reached out of nowhere to wring her stomach with a painful mixture of embarrassment and fear.

What on earth? The room was empty.

Then her glance fell on the solid-backed settle she'd already noticed. "You should rather blush at being exposed as a sneak and an eavesdropper, Lord Bruard," she said, too upset to guard her tongue.

Instead of the apology he owed her, the response was a soft chuckle that played forbidden music up and down her spine. "You recognize my voice. I'm flattered."

"You're the only Scotsman in the party," she said stiffly, bending to pick up the book. It was a first edition. It deserved better than her flinging it to the floor.

In fact, she was the one blushing. Because while it was true that a trace of the earl's northern roots was audible in his speech, she didn't recognize his voice because of his accent. She recognized his voice because ever since she'd arrived at this house, she'd dreamed of him. In her fantasies, that insolent baritone whispered wicked suggestions that turned her nights to fire.

"Cruel beauty. I hoped you'd noticed me, yet now you depress my pretensions."

"I couldn't miss noticing you," she said in an even icier tone. "You're notorious."

"I am indeed." He didn't sound like he considered that any cause for remorse. "Is that why you've been avoiding me, Mrs. Martin? For fear my reputation might corrupt your upstanding morals?"

Oh, dear. She had been avoiding him. But the knowledge that he'd noticed her skittishness was somehow threatening.

"There's nothing wrong with my morals," she said hotly, before she reminded herself that a silent and immediate departure from the library was the wisest path.

"More is the pity."

It seemed that she was in no mood to be wise. Clutching the book, she marched around the settle to confront him. "Lord Bruard, you…"

"Yes?" He was stretched full-length against the cushions, as relaxed and dangerous as a big cat. Not a lion or a tiger. There was nothing golden about his saturnine beauty. A panther, perhaps.

"A gentleman would have made his presence known." She hated how prim and stuffy she sounded.

A lazy smile curled his long, rather cruel mouth and set his dark eyes glittering. "I'm sure a gentleman would."

He paused for her to make the connection that he wasn't a gentleman. She didn't need reminding, God help her.

As the smile deepened, a jolt of unwelcome attraction struck her like lightning. But how could she help it? Lord Bruard was almost sinfully beautiful, with his thick black hair and thin face, all cheekbones and jaw and long, aquiline nose. He looked like a fallen angel. She had no doubt that he'd sinned enough to merit damnation.

Without any conviction, Selina told herself that her response to his presence was no great matter. Any woman with blood in her veins would thrill to the way he looked. It was a natural reaction.

But the woeful truth was that she'd been responding for a week. She'd never felt like this before, like she was a stand of dry timber – and Lord Bruard was a blazing torch, primed to send her up in roaring flames. She'd reminded herself over and over that too many other women felt exactly the same, and if she had any pride she'd stifle this unwilling fascination. Good heavens, even Lady Derwent's eighty-year-old maiden aunt went all silly and giggly at the sight of this infamous rake.

Selina's existence had been grim and purposeful. The only happiness she'd ever known was founded in her love for her son. She'd never before fallen prey to an irresistible attraction. And to such an unworthy object, at that. She was disgusted with herself.

Although no amount of disgust changed the way the mere sound of the Scottish earl's voice made her skin tighten in desire and her heart race with excitement.

He went on in a musing tone. "But if I had announced my presence, I'd have missed out on overhearing a very interesting conversation."

Interesting? His definition of the word must differ from hers. "Your entertainment trumps good manners?"

"Naturally my entertainment is paramount."

She shouldn't find his complete lack of shame appealing. But she'd spent her life overburdened with rules and restrictions, and Bruard's contempt for social niceties was alluring.

Devil take him, everything about him was alluring. She'd never met an out-and-out wrong 'un before. She'd never wasted her time thinking about handsome, idle, dissipated men. If she had, she would assume that her overdeveloped sense of right and wrong meant she'd abominate them. She'd certainly had no patience for her late husband's attempts to ape the excesses of the upper classes.

What an innocent she'd been until she met Lord Bruard. One dismissive glance from those fathomless dark green eyes under their sweep of thick lashes, and all she wanted to do was get closer.

Much closer.

If she had an ounce of principle, she should despise Bruard. Cecil certainly did. Alone with Selina, he'd spent hours railing against the Derwents for daring to pollute the pure air of their country house with the sinner's presence.

Selina didn't despise Bruard. She wanted him. At night in her empty bed, she touched herself and imagined that the hands on her skin weren't small and soft, but large and tanned and skilled, and that a deep, drawling voice murmured profane encouragement in her ears.

Memory of those forbidden moments assailed her now and made her blush again. She was too aware that it was late and that she was alone with a man whose reputation was bad enough to send respectable virgins shrieking for their mammas. Lord Bruard's company was the closest thing to satanic temptation that she was ever likely to experience.

Selina swallowed to moisten a dry throat and set the book on the mantel with a shaking hand. "I must go," she said, and cursed the squeak in her voice.

"Must you?" Bruard didn't sound as though he cared whether she stayed or not. He continued as though they were in the middle of a friendly conversation. "You shouldn't let him bully you, you know. If he bullies you now, before he gets his ring on your finger, he'll turn into a domestic tyrant when you marry."

She paused in the act of turning away toward the door. "This is none of your business, sir."

Unfortunately, it was also an accurate assessment of her future. Selina was no fool, and she didn't deceive herself about how life with Cecil would turn out. But what choice did she have?

With a leisurely grace that made her foolish heart skip around inside her tight chest, Bruard sat up. She thought she'd committed her whole self to marrying Cecil, but now it turned out that her heart hadn't signed up to the arrangement. Her heart cried out that she was still young and at last she had the chance to flirt with an attractive man. It insisted that if she ran away, she was a filthy coward.

"That's true." Again no shame. "But I'm telling you this out of pure altruism. Stand up for yourself now, or he'll crush every ounce of spirit out of you."

"Pure altruism?" Her snort of amusement would have shocked Cecil. "It seems the world is completely wrong about you, Lord Bruard."

The half-smile reappeared, accentuating the creases around Bruard's deep-set eyes. The breath jammed in her lungs. Lord above, no wonder the ladies went insane for him. His appeal was extraordinary. He should have warning signs posted all over him.

Because he was right about her avoiding him, this was closer than she'd ever ventured to the wicked Lord Bruard. This was certainly the longest that she'd spent talking to him.

And danger bristled in the air.

So remaining in this room made no sense. Yet remain Selina did.

He fixed a disturbingly assessing gaze on her. "No, my lovely little ghost, the world isn't wrong about me."

The power of his attraction made her stomach cramp with nerves, as she remembered all those depraved fantasies that had worn Lord Bruard's intense dark face. Did he know that she'd thought of him in the privacy of the night? She had a sick feeling that he must.

"G-ghost?" she stammered.

He shrugged. How could such a prosaic movement make her heart somersault? Except his shoulders were broad and hard, and she ached to run her hands along them and down those strong arms, displayed to advantage in the best of London tailoring.

He wore black. But then didn't the devil always come in black?

"That's how I think of you. With your neat little gray frocks, and the way you watch every word you say, and never miss anything that goes on around you."

This time, genuine fear spurred her unsteady pulse. She hadn't thought that she'd be of the slightest interest to such a libertine. It turned out she was wrong. It seemed that just as she'd watched him, he'd watched her.

Selina gulped for air to clear a swimming head and raised an unsteady hand to her bosom, before she realized how revealing the movement was. "You shouldn't think of me at all."

His gaze grew more focused, and she faltered back a step. She should flee, pride or no pride, but it was as if her feet were tacked to the parquetry floor.

"Nor should you think of me, when you're marrying that ponderous oaf in a fortnight, and you're obviously a woman who guards her chastity the way a miser guards his gold."

Heat blazed in her cheeks, and she avoided his eyes. How could he make her virtue sound like the worst of sins? "I don't think of you. I..."

Oh, what was the use? All of a sudden, coyness seemed too shabby to countenance. As he uncoiled and rose to his feet, Selina made a helpless gesture. "I don't want to think of you," she mumbled.

His soft purr reeked of satisfaction. Selina raised her gaze to his face, expecting smugness, but he stared at her as if he tracked every beat of her heart. Heaven help her, he probably did.

A man this experienced with women must register her terrified fascination. The fact that she'd tried so hard to keep out of his way told its own story to someone who paid close attention. To her astonished dismay, Bruard had paid close attention.

He was tall and all whipcord strength. She wasn't a small woman, but he towered over her. "That is no doubt true. But sometimes it's impossible to obey common sense, isn't it?"

"How would you know?" she asked with a trace of heat. She started to resent feeling like a butterfly caught on a collector's pin.

"*Brava*." To her surprise, this time he smiled properly. "I knew there was more to you than, 'Yes, Cecil.'"

Reminder of her duty forced a guilty gasp from her. "I shouldn't be talking to you."

Cecil would have a fit if he caught her alone with this debauchee. Even if someone came in and discovered her with Bruard, the story would be sure to reach him.

Selina turned once more to go, while some heretofore silent corner of her soul pleaded with her to remain. This short, spiky conversation with Lord Bruard counted as the most exciting thing that had ever happened to her. And wasn't that an indictment on a dull, wasted life?

"No, you shouldn't." He reached out and caught her arm. "But all the same, I'd like you to stay."

Heat sizzled up her arm and down through her middle until it settled in a great molten lump in the pit of her stomach. "Let me go," Selina muttered, cringing to hear how her voice wavered.

"Stay. Please."

Shocked, she stopped in her tracks and stared up at him. "You don't sound like you say please very often."

Self-derisive humor glinted in his eyes. "I don't."

He kept hold of her arm. If his touch had been demanding or possessive, she'd have jerked away. But it was gentle as a man's hand never was when it touched her. She told herself Bruard knew the power of gentleness and he used it against her. But even conceding that, the contact was so sweet, she couldn't bring herself to pull free.

"I can't see why I've caught your eye," she said in bewilderment.

"Can't you?" he said in a neutral voice.

"Is it because I've tried so hard to stay away from you?"

She'd noticed the ladies at this large house party were inclined to cluster around him. He'd never looked very interested. But then the first thing she'd noticed about him, apart from his spectacular looks, was the air of boredom that hung about him. She suspected too much had come to him too easily, and life lost its flavor.

He was from a great Scottish family. He was rich. Lovers vied to share his bed. He drew women to him, without having to lift the little finger on that elegant hand. No wonder he looked as if the whole wide world was a complete yawn.

Except one of the most unsettling elements of this unsettling encounter was that right now, he didn't look bored at all. Right now, he bristled with purpose. She'd likened him to a drowsing panther. Now she'd awoken the big cat, and he was on the hunt.

Mad as it seemed, his quarry was frumpy, undistinguished Selina Martin. Of all tonight's surprises, that had to be the greatest.

"No. I noticed you the moment you set foot in this house." The purposeful look he sent her blasted another bolt of heat from her crown to her toes in their satin slippers. His grip tightened on her arm. "Just as you noticed me."

It was true. They'd gone past the point where she could deny it.

She remained trembling in his grasp, a host of giant grasshoppers leaping around in her stomach.

"Yes." The word was a mere breath.

Selina waited for triumph, for Bruard to sweep her into his arms. Because surely her reckless confession must beggar restraint. She almost wished he would act the way she expected a Lothario to act. All grabby hands and slobbery kisses.

If he took her admission as a signal for seizing her, she might summon up the will to leave. But those hard, long-fingered hands didn't grab, and that thin, expressive mouth didn't slobber.

A light glittered in his green eyes. "Are you really going to marry that clodhopping dunderhead?"

"He's...he's not a dunderhead. He's one of the cleverest men in England."

At least when it came to making money. Cecil had mills all over the north of England, and coalmines and a fleet of ships. All built up from a modest inheritance from his yeoman father. Cecil, by rights, wasn't wellborn enough to socialize with the Derwents and their circle, but Lord Derwent was seeking investment in an iron foundry. Money talked louder than breeding, however much the other guests made it clear that Cecil and his dowdy fiancée were here only on sufferance.

"I don't believe it. If he is, he has no idea how to handle a woman. Especially a woman as exquisite as the one he's caught."

Exquisite? Nobody had ever called her that before. During her life, most of the vanity had been beaten out of her. But praise from such a connoisseur of beauty would spark pleasure in even the world's most self-effacing lady.

All pleasure fled when Lord Bruard went on. "Give the sod his marching orders. You're too fine for him."

Horrid reality crashed down over her like a wave of freezing cold seawater. She might be too fine for Cecil, but she was too poor to think of giving him his marching orders. She broke away from Lord Bruard and slumped down onto the settle.

"Is becoming your mistress a better option?" Bitterness edged her voice, although she wasn't angry with Bruard. Not really. "I doubt it."

Selina was however furious with herself. She knew what was at stake in her engagement to Cecil. Too much to risk everything on a flirtation with a rake, bored with easy conquests.

Bruard would get bored with her, too. Right now, she'd captured his interest because she'd tried to stay out of his way. Once he'd had her, any novelty would soon wear off. And with the novelty, whatever obscure charm he saw in her.

He didn't try to take her arm again. "Perhaps you should wait until I ask you."

"I'm inexperienced with dalliance." She gave him a direct look. "But this feels like you're getting ready to invite me into your bed."

His laugh held a note of reluctant admiration. "By heaven, you're brave. I've already seen so much in you, so much that every other idiot here has missed, but I didn't see that."

Selina didn't warm to the backhanded compliment. "Have I got this wrong? You're not asking me to sleep with you?"

That sensual smile curled his lips once more. "I had more in mind than sleeping, but, no, you haven't got it wrong."

Her mind exploded with a thousand glorious ways Lord Bruard could fill her nights. Longing knotted her stomach – and regret, because she couldn't say yes. Not when she had Gerald to worry about.

"I have to marry Cecil," she said in an uncompromising tone.

Her conscience told her to leave the library. Instead, she leaned against the back of the settle. She'd never have another chance to be alone with an attractive man. The temptation to linger overcame self-preservation. In the barren years to come, she'd take out her memory of this night and treasure it. For one glittering moment, she'd wanted a man and he'd wanted her in return.

Lord Bruard regarded her with displeasure. The expression made him look like a sulky pasha, unimpressed with the seraglio's offerings. "Because he's rich, I suppose."

Her lips tightened, although it would do her no good to deny the truth. "I assume you despise me for that."

"It was ever thus." He shrugged. "Gold buys beauty. Beauty buys gold. No, I don't despise you."

Because she saw he was sincere, whereas she very much despised her mercenary motives, she explained, and devil take discretion. "I'm not far off indigent. My late husband was a gambler. And I have a son to care for."

He sighed and ran his hand through that disheveled mass of silky, dark hair. "I understand."

"Do you?"

"Of course. But even with all his riches, you must be able to do better than Canley-Smythe."

Bleak humor twisted her lips. "I'm a poor widow with no influential connections. How many fabulously wealthy men do you think swim into my acquaintance? How many even moderately solvent men? Beggars can't be choosers, Lord Bruard. A beggar I'll be, if I don't go through with this wedding on Boxing Day."

After all this time, it was a relief to be honest. Even if the last person she'd ever imagined she'd confide in was a man notorious throughout the land for his sexual exploits.

But Lord Bruard spoke to her as if she was human, as if she had a brain in her head, and her shocking confession of marrying for money hadn't repelled him.

"I'm sorry," he said in a quiet voice.

"Because I'm not free to throw myself into your unreliable arms?" Again that hint of anger.

"My arms are perfectly reliable." His marked black brows rose. "It's my character that you can't trust."

She released a huff of shocked laughter. "You're honest at least."

"I can't see the point of being anything else."

He sat beside her. He wasn't close enough to crowd her, but his nearness sent desire prickling across her skin. "Did you love the late Mr. Martin?"

"Love seems an odd word on your lips."

He shrugged. "Humor me."

"Why?" Baffled, she spread her hands. "You must know your wiles are wasted on me."

Bruard leaned back and stretched his long legs toward the fire. He folded his arms over his chest and went back to looking like a sleepy panther. "You leave me to worry about my wiles, Mrs. Martin."

Selina stared down into her lap where her hands twisted together in an agitated dance. She waited for Bruard to pursue the question about Roderick, but he seemed content to remain silent. And because he was patient – a quality lacking in most of the men she knew – in the end, she answered.

"No, I didn't love him." Her voice was low, and her hands clenched around each other.

When Lord Bruard didn't respond, she found herself explaining. "My parents arranged the marriage. Roderick's father was a well-to-do merchant in Lichfield. My father was a doctor in a village outside the town. He was much older than my mother and not well, so when he saw a chance to settle my future, he took it."

"How old were you?"

"Just seventeen. Papa died a month after the wedding. I'm sad that he never got to meet my son Gerald. They're very alike." As always when she thought of her son, the weight in her heart eased, so her words emerged more smoothly. "But I'm glad Papa never knew that he'd given me to a man who was a faithless drunkard and a wastrel. I had nine years of unhappiness with Roderick."

"I'm sorry," Bruard said again.

She turned to study the earl. On paper, he was cut from the same cloth as Roderick. Except he wasn't. Bruard possessed a strength and integrity that her husband had never come close to owning. Bruard was the kind of man Roderick had aspired to be, but instead her husband had never grown beyond being a spoiled child.

"So am I."

Bruard regarded her with grave eyes. "I'm particularly sorry that you've never known an ounce of joy."

Damn her for these maudlin confessions. Her pride revolted at the idea of Lord Bruard pitying her. "I was a happy child, if a little lonely. I had no brothers and sisters, because Mamma was delicate.

It's one of my great regrets that Gerald is also an only child."

"Unless you and Cecil have children."

She struggled to mask a grimace at the thought of the making of those children. "Yes."

Cecil wanted sons. He'd told her.

She could endure it. For Gerald's sake, she could endure anything.

When she saw that she hadn't managed to conceal her distaste, she rushed on. "And I love my son. There's joy in that."

"I'm sure." Bruard's discontented expression persisted. "But that's the mother's joy. What about the woman's?"

Every drop of moisture dried from her mouth. She'd been frank with him, way beyond what their short acquaintance justified. Now she should tell him to mind his own business, but she found herself revealing the truth in an embarrassed mutter. "I've never known it."

Which wasn't entirely true, she admitted in silent mortification. Although while the touch of her hand might ease her aching frustration, it never came close to joy.

"You'll never know it with Canley-Smythe. And you're the sort of woman who won't take a lover, once you've pledged your faith to the blockhead."

"He's not a blockhead," she said, cursing her hesitation. When Lord Bruard didn't reply, she went on with a trace of desperation. "You seem to imagine you know me."

That cursed alluring smile curled his lips again. "Did you ever play that reprobate Roderick Martin false, despite his infidelities?"

Heat rose in her cheeks, as if she was about to confess some misdeed. When it was just the opposite. "No, of course not."

"You'll be just as faithful to old moneybags."

"You make that sound like a bad thing," she protested.

"When a beautiful, spirited creature like you submits to a clod like Cecil Canley-Smythe, it *is* a bad thing."

Selina stared appalled at Bruard. "You haven't been watching me as closely as I thought. Nobody in their right mind would describe me as spirited. The ladies at this house party call me the dullest woman in England. I've heard them say it."

To her surprise, he looked angry. "Toplofty little bitches."

She should object to his language, but she'd suffered too many snubs from the nasty cats to waste time defending them. "I am the most boring woman in England. I stay where I'm put, and I do what I'm told."

Bitterness edged her tone, because it had always struck her as the waste of a life. The only worthwhile thing she'd ever done was give birth to Gerald.

He looked thoughtful. "You don't have to follow the rules all the time."

She slid along the settle to lengthen the distance between them. "I'm not throwing over my engagement for the sake of your smile, Lord Bruard, however charming it might be."

He surveyed her as if he could read every inch of her soul. Selina had an uncanny feeling that, despite her taunts, he had come to understand her over the last week. Then she reminded herself that he was a rake, and he knew just what to say to a woman to win her over.

"I could show you joy," he said in a soft voice that played more of that devil's music up and down her backbone.

"I'm sure you could," she said flatly. "But I won't let you seduce me in Lord Derwent's library, where anyone could come in and discover us."

"It would put paid to your reputation for dullness, at least."

Despite everything, she laughed. "You're incorrigible."

"I am." He paused, and his expression grew so intense that fear made her breath accelerate. "Anyway, my ambitions reach further than that. I want more of you than one hurried tumble in another man's house, before the servants come in to snuff the candles."

"You must know that's impossible. I've told you what's at stake." Selina paused, feeling let down. Which was stupid. The world knew Brock Drummond, the Earl of Bruard, was a wicked man. She couldn't complain when he lived up to his reputation. "You seemed to understand my dilemma. Or was all that compassion just a libertine's trick, so I'd let you have your way with me?"

Surprise lit his dark eyes. And something that looked like appreciation. "You don't mince your words, do you?"

Suddenly weary, she stared into the fire. "What's the point?"

"None that I can see, but most ladies wouldn't agree." She wasn't looking at him, but she could hear that he was smiling. "How on earth does anyone think you're dull?"

"I mind my tongue most of the time. I should have minded my tongue tonight."

"That would have been a pity."

She stood and smoothed her skirts. This had gone far enough. Since they'd started talking, danger had flickered in the air. Now it flapped around her with huge, black wings.

"I should go to bed. Alone." In case Bruard imagined that was an invitation. "It's been an entertaining encounter, my lord."

He rose to face her, his expression intent. "To Hades with that. Do you dare to dismiss me like an importunate creditor, madam? I'll be damned if you will."

Startled, she stared at him. She faltered back. "I told you I can't..."

He sounded annoyed. "No, you can't tonight. But for the next two weeks, Cecil is safe in the north and you're within reach in the south, and I find myself at your disposal."

"To do what?"

"Why, to show you what you've been missing."

His smile made him look a complete scoundrel. Selina shivered with nerves, and with the force of the attraction assailing her. When he seized her hand, the contact blasted her like fire.

She regarded him in consternation and tried to pull away. "It's impossible. Even if I wanted to say yes, Gerald comes home from school in a week."

"Then give me a week. A week when you come to me as my willing lover. A week when you're not Roderick Martin's neglected wife or Cecil Canley-Smythe's obedient helpmeet." His voice lowered into an enthralling murmur. "A week when you're Selina, the woman I desire above all others."

CHAPTER TWO

*B*rock watched that lovely face freeze in shock. He braced for her to pull away, for her to protest that she was a good woman and his improper proposal offended her. Even the most round-heeled wench liked to demur to dispel any impression that she was an easy conquest. And Selina Martin was no lightskirt. She was the kind of chaste, principled woman he usually ran a mile to avoid.

Since he'd first seen this demure widow, all calm control and subtle shades of old gold, he'd told himself over and over to forget his inconvenient fascination. It had done no good. She haunted him as no woman ever had. While she wasn't his usual quarry, he refused to accept that she wasn't for him.

As so often tonight, she surprised him. "You make it sound so tempting."

No coy denials. No vacillating between yes and no, when the answer was always yes. Brock had become bored with easy victories. Yet here it seemed Selina considered his proposition a mere moment and the answer wasn't no, and still he could barely contain his excitement.

He smiled, hoping he didn't look half-witted with delight. He stepped closer. "I thought you'd slap my face."

"I should." The uncertain curve of her lips hinted that she was unused to smiling and wasn't sure if it was allowed.

She never smiled when she was with the lout she was engaged to. Whenever she mentioned her son, she smiled. If Brock got her to himself, he'd make sure she smiled all the time.

She firmed her grip on his hand. His heart gave a mighty thump. Dear God, she was holding his *hand,* and he was about to go up in flames. He hadn't been in such a lather about a female since he was a lad. Not even then.

Selina went on in a low voice. "I'm not nearly so proper as I like to pretend I am."

Oh? Now that was intriguing. "So you'll do this?"

"I should say no. It's mad that I'm even considering it."

"This is our chance, Selina. Don't pass it up because you're afraid."

She gave a choked laugh and to his regret tugged her hand free. "I am afraid."

"And interested?"

"And interested." She studied him with a worried frown. "But how would we manage it? I have to marry Cecil after Christmas, and I can't let any harm come to Gerald. If you know of a way that we can do this safely, I'd like to hear it."

Brock gave a shout of laughter and threw himself back onto the settle. "You're magnificent, Selina. More magnificent even than I thought, and I've spent the week wondering why nobody else has marked what an extraordinary treasure you are."

She frowned, deep brown eyes still troubled. His extravagant praise didn't ease her concerns, he could see. "I still don't understand why you would."

"Don't you?"

When she sat beside him, he settled his gaze on her. He'd watched her all week, careful not to attract the other guests' attention. It was a relief and a pleasure to stare at her and drink his full.

"No, I don't. I truly am as dull as everyone believes. If we do this reckless thing, you're going to end up being frightfully disappointed."

He laughed again on a gentler note, and cupped her cheek in one hand. She started under his touch but didn't pull away. "I doubt it. You're the most enchanting creature I've ever met. And the most elusive."

Her lips turned down. "That's what I fear. The lure of the chase made you notice me. Now I've stopped running, you'll decide I wasn't worth hunting in the first place."

"You make me sound like a cat torturing a mouse," he protested.

When her eyes ate him up, possessive yearning twisted his gut. He knew Selina had no idea that whenever she looked at him, her gaze sharpened with carnal hunger. He'd caught this avid expression a few times, and every time he'd ached to seize her in his arms and tell the curious world to go to hell.

"There's something a little cruel about you, Lord Bruard."

"Brock."

She hadn't objected when he called her Selina. Now he watched her delicate features soften. When she spoke his name, it sounded like a benediction. "Brock."

Tenderness sliced through him, sharp as a knife, and he leaned in to kiss her. He kept enough grip on strategy to rein in his passion – although passion stirred as powerful as a dragon waking in its cave.

She made a faint sound of surprise, and her lips fluttered beneath his. She tasted like honey. She kissed like an untried maiden. For a burning second, sweetness overwhelmed him.

Brock wasn't a man who did sweetness. Or tenderness. But something about this slender woman with her dark blond hair and sad eyes sparked protective instincts that he hadn't known he possessed.

She pulled back. Which was probably a good thing. Because now wasn't the time to push her to greater intimacies. The settle concealed them from the doorway, but as she said, anyone could come in. If they were discovered alone like this, it would cause scandal enough. If they were kissing, the fat would truly hit the fire.

He dropped his hand from her face. In part because he hadn't counted on the heady effect of touching her. During this house party, he'd slept alone, despite plenty of opportunities for company. But compared to Selina Martin's refined beauty, every other woman here seemed overblown and obvious.

As Selina raised a trembling hand to touch her lush lips, her eyes were round with astonishment. He had plans for those lips, plans that had kept him randy and restless all week. How could a woman with a mouth made for sin imagine that any man could find her disappointing?

"That was…"

"A promise of more to come." He caught her hand again. Now he'd touched her, it was impossible to stop. "Will you give me a week, Selina?"

"You'd need to promise discretion. Word can never get out that we were together."

"I swear I'll never speak of this."

"Thank you."

"So will you come to me?"

That hungry gaze roamed his features, making his blood churn with heat. "If I can."

Triumph surged through him. It was yes. By God, it was yes.

He spoke in a rush, in case she changed her mind. "I have a hunting box in the Essex marshes. Lovely and isolated. Even better, it's only a couple of hours away. I don't want to spend days stuck in a carriage."

Although he could think of plenty of things that they could do in a carriage. A week wasn't long enough for everything that he wanted to experience with this woman.

But a week was all they had. There was no point regretting their limited time together. He never wasted energy fretting over impossibilities.

Brock went on. "You'll love it. The sea is only a mile away."

Her eyes glowed with anticipation. "I've never seen the sea."

He dared to tease her. Now he had her consent, he was ready to dare his life. "I hope it's not just the sightseeing you find appealing."

To his surprise, Selina smiled, properly this time. "I look forward to seeing the country. Not to mention a certain wicked gentleman who may offer a modicum of entertainment."

He laughed. He'd never imagined her mocking him. Hell, he wanted to kiss her again, but he couldn't risk it. If she came to him tomorrow, he'd kiss her until she was breathless.

"We can't leave Derwent Hall together," she said. "And I brought a maid with me. What can I do with her? I don't want her coming with us, but I'll have to tell her something."

"Can you make up some reason not to go home straightaway? A school friend or a relative in the area you'd like to see?"

"I suppose I could." She made a moue of self-disgust. "I'm not used to telling lies."

"Will you lie this once for me, Selina?"

She looked down to where he held her hand. "Gladly." The eyes she raised to his were brilliant with light. "I'll say that I have a friend who lives nearby. I'm lying on my own behalf, too. I want to know how it feels to share my body with a man I want, not one to whom I owe no more than duty."

Poignant emotion clogged his throat – when he wasn't a man who did emotion either – and his voice emerged as a rasp. "You do me too much honor, my darling."

While he'd called a host of women his darling, Brock had an inkling that when he called Selina his darling, he meant it.

His desire for her was compelling, but he was familiar with desire. Woefully so, the judgmental world would say. But something in this quiet room swept him, the infamous libertine, out from shore and into uncharted waters. For one fraught moment, he wondered if Selina Martin was more dangerous to him than he could imagine and perhaps he'd be wise to stay away from her.

But as he stared into her delicate face, wisdom was a word that held no power.

"There's an inn on the London road called the Blue Wagon. I'll leave before breakfast and wait for you there. Come as soon as you can. I resent every moment that we're apart."

Selina continued to look troubled. Her light brown brows, several shades darker than that thick honey-colored hair, drew together. "I'll send my maid on to London. We're packing up the house, so I can make some excuse for wanting a bit of peace and quiet in the country. She's been with me since I was a girl. Even if she suspects my motives for staying in Essex, she won't betray me. I'll arrange for my carriage to return after our time is over."

Damn it all, Brock didn't want to think about that. Not now when he had a week of unequaled pleasure stretching before him. "Something is worrying you. Tell me."

That was new, too. As a rule, Brock preferred his lovers to keep their thoughts to themselves. The awful truth was that in most cases, his paramours were far too eager to unburden their hearts into his ears.

Selina had always been mysterious. Her reticence was among the many aspects of her personality that he found attractive. Now he burned to discover all her secrets.

Patience, laddie. You've got a week ahead.

She looked surprised at his demand. "It's just..."

"Yes?"

She freed her hand and made a helpless gesture. "It all seems so random. By chance, Cecil and I came in here to discuss our arrangements for tomorrow. By chance, you overheard us. If some other lady had ventured into the library, would you have made the same offer to her?"

Brock couldn't help it. He caught her face between his hands and kissed her swift and hard. "No. On my honor, no. I knew you were mine, the moment I saw you. I'd already planned to pursue you to London. This encounter just presented me with an opportunity I intended to create anyway."

Once she stopped looking dazzled, she looked relieved. "I don't want you to take my consent cheaply. I said yes too fast, I know, but we don't have time for games."

That extraordinary tenderness cramped his heart again. "I'm aware of the privilege you grant me."

"You're so good at words." Her gaze roamed across his face. "Words are easy."

He struggled not to squirm under her perceptive inspection. Because she was right. Words were easy, and he'd used them so often to persuade a reluctant lady of his sincerity, when he intended nothing past a quick fuck.

"If I say I mean it this time, you'll only suggest that's what I always say."

Wry humor curved her lips. "And is it?"

"Aye." He lifted her hand and brushed a kiss across the knuckles before he let her go. "You'll just have to trust me."

She had that dazed look in her eyes that appeared whenever he touched her. He loved that this attraction between them made dissimulation impossible.

"It's mad, but despite how short a time I've known you, despite..."

"My reputation," he said grimly, because he was too aware of what people said about him. He was even more aware that most of it was justified.

The strange thing was that only as he looked into Selina's deep brown eyes did he feel any shame for his riotous ways, the lies he'd told, the hearts he'd broken. Because he found himself caught in the liar's dilemma. He told the truth, yet nobody with half a brain would believe him.

Selina didn't flinch from what he was. He came to realize that she was the bravest woman he'd ever met. When he'd first seen her, he recognized straightaway that she didn't love that lumbering yokel Cecil Canley-Smythe. Brock was in no position to criticize her for marrying for money. But before tonight, he'd imagined that he pursued a woman slightly less principled than she turned out to be.

Now he realized the sacrifice she made for her boy. She was under no illusions about Cecil, but she was willing to pay any price in return for her son's security. Brock's mother had been vain and flighty and selfish. Selina's stalwart maternal love left him in awe.

"Yes, there's your reputation. But that's part of your appeal."

Startled, he let out a bark of laughter and stretched one arm along the top of the settle behind her. "The devil you say."

"You're perfect, Lord Bruard."

Before they were done, she'd call him Brock without thinking about it. "Just who is seducing whom in this scene, madam?"

She smiled, her eyes sparkling. He hadn't expected this impish humor either. "I caught you in my trap."

"That you have." Many a true word was spoken in jest. "I'm not sure I've ever been called perfect before."

That fugitive pink heated her cheeks again. He'd never before found himself so enchanted by the sheer wealth of detail he discovered in a woman.

"Let's not go too far. I'm not saying you're perfect for anything except my purposes. But it's your sins that make you the ideal candidate to share my bed."

"You want to conquer the rake?" He couldn't contain the cynicism edging the question. And a hint of disappointment. He knew that many women pursued him to discover what all the fuss was about. He hadn't put Selina Martin in that category.

"I've given myself to only one man, and he didn't satisfy me. I can't imagine that Cecil will be much better. If I'm to kick over the traces just once in my life, I want it to be with a man who knows what he's doing. I've had enough clumsy fumbling."

He winced at her frank description. What a crying shame that this glorious creature had never found a lover to match her.

Until now.

She went on. "I don't want a man who asks more of me than I can give. I don't want someone who sees this as a love affair and who will be hurt or jealous when I leave him to marry Cecil. The rakish Lord Bruard won't start imagining that what we do together is any more significant than two adults who fancy each other deciding to spend a week together."

Brock was piqued, despite her pragmatism mirroring the usual arrangement he offered a lover. But in the past, the declaration of noninvolvement came from him, not from his partner in pleasure.

He should appreciate Selina's candor. Ridiculous, but he didn't. In fact this revelation that Selina felt nothing but an itch she'd like to scratch left him feeling...hurt.

Hurt was another reaction outside his ken. Again, some instinct warned him that this quiet widow posed a risk to the man he'd always been.

His voice was sharp as he responded. "I hope this will be more than a fleshly transaction. I hope we can share respect and friendship."

She went back to looking startled. "Do you?"

"Don't you?"

She regarded him as if she'd cracked open a chicken egg and a baby unicorn had popped out onto her breakfast plate. "I assumed you'd be so inured to temporary liaisons, you wouldn't seek an...emotional connection."

So had he.

"Damn it, Selina, I like you." With an irritated exhalation, he ran his hand through his hair. Although he suspected he was more annoyed with himself than with her. "I want you, of course I do, but I feel more for you than the simple urge to fuck you. I hoped you might like me, too."

For pity's sake, he started to sound like a needy boy, and he hadn't needed anyone since he'd realized the world offered him a cornucopia of pleasure and no deeper connections at all.

Her pause before she answered irked him more than it should. "I don't know you."

He lowered his arm from the back of the settle and clenched his hand on his thigh. "You know me well enough to offer me your body."

She frowned at him. "You could make a nun swoon with yearning. Do I need to like you? I want you, too."

Her bald declaration of desire crashed through him like a blow. But while that had always been enough from his other lovers, from Selina Martin, he wanted more. "Do you really only see me as a walking cock?"

The pink in her cheeks deepened, but she didn't look away. "It would be best if you were." Her hands spread in bewilderment. "Are you...are you considering changing your mind?"

Not on his life. "Are you?"

"No." Although she didn't sound certain. "I'm sorry I misjudged you. I only had the gossip to go on, you see."

"Gossip says if it moves, I'll fuck it."

"You...you're very frank."

"Does it offend you?"

"No."

Brock had to lean closer to hear. The scent of jasmine filled his head. It was a more sensual scent than he thought she'd choose, but this astonishing conversation revealed she harbored depths he'd never suspected.

"It's exciting." She went on, her voice a mere whisper. "Nobody has ever spoken to me like this. Roderick was a bit of a prude. He hardly ever mentioned our relations. And it's not a subject that I've broached with Cecil."

"He wants you." Brock had seen that from the first.

"Yes," she said with a commendable lack of false modesty. "That's why he's prepared to take on a penniless widow with a son. He's rich enough to look much higher for a bride, perhaps even to the aristocracy."

Selina was no dupe. Nor was she a coy ingénue, for all her lack of experience with sexual satisfaction. Brock had started the night wanting her. Now he was in a fever to have her to himself.

"You're the one who stoops to accept him."

Self-mockery twisted her lips. "The world wouldn't agree."

"The world is an ass." Brock returned to what was worrying him. "You trust me enough to consent to be my lover."

Another of those searching inspections that seemed to penetrate to his stained soul. "Yes, I do. I don't know why, but something tells me I'm in safe hands."

Warmth filled him, although God knew he was no hero. "I'll do my best to justify your faith."

"I only ask you to be careful. I don't love Cecil, but I owe him better than to marry him already carrying another man's child."

Brock curled his hand over the back of the settle to stop himself from reaching for her. "I'll be as careful as I can be."

"That's all I ask."

Anticipation filled Brock, made his blood fizz like champagne. "So we have a rendezvous tomorrow at the Blue Wagon?"

Determination hardened her features. "We do."

"Then it's time we parted." He stood and held out his hand. "I promised to keep you from scandal. We've been lucky that nobody has come in to discover us."

"I doubt Lord Derwent's guests are interested in the library," she said drily.

Her humor drew a huff of appreciative laughter from Brock. He was sure she was right. The house party had passed in drinking and gossip and sex – with Canley-Smythe and his prim betrothed distinctly out of place in the louche atmosphere. "Lucky for me I wandered in for a moment's quiet reflection, then."

A moment alone, so he could plot his seduction of Cecil Canley-Smythe's future wife, more like. It turned out that no plotting had been necessary. Tonight, it was clear that the devil was on his side.

"Lucky for me." She took his hand and rose, then her upward movement continued.

Only as her arms slid around his neck and she stretched to fit her lips to his did he realize what she intended. He, the great seducer, caught out by a beautiful woman's boldness. The press of her body made him as hard as a wooden spar.

But her lips were soft and eager and tasted of an innocence that belied her widowhood. Her awkward fervor made his head spin. Dear Lord above, she even kept her mouth closed like a young girl kissed for the first time.

All night, Selina had held him suspended almost painfully between tenderness and desire. Why should her kiss be any different?

It was slow to dawn on him that this woman who had been married for nine years and borne a child had no idea how to kiss a man. Tonight he'd heard enough to learn to despise Roderick Martin. Now he wished the bugger was alive so that he could murder him. The bastard had had the supreme good fortune to marry Selina, yet from what Brock could see, he hadn't put an ounce of effort into cherishing her.

So the hands that curled around her waist were gentle, not urgent with possession. Brock used his lips to temper her untutored enthusiasm. When he flicked his tongue along the seam of her lips, she released a soft sound of astonishment. He repeated the action more slowly and sucked her lower lip into his mouth, laving it with his tongue. She tasted glorious, and another of those confused little hums of pleasure sent arousal thundering through him.

When he pulled back, she gave a gratifying growl of disappointment. He trailed kisses down the side of her face. "Open for me, Selina."

She went rigid in his hold. "Open?"

He pressed his lips to hers, and this time nipped at that luscious lower lip. When she parted to allow him entry, he felt like he'd won a mighty victory. With leisurely enjoyment, he swept his tongue into the warm, wet heat of her mouth.

Selina shuddered on a confused murmur. This symphony of incoherent moans and sighs was damnably stirring. He wanted to hear her when he thrust deep inside her, when he brought her to climax.

Not tonight. But soon.

He remained aware of their danger, even as she lost herself in the kiss. He drew her down onto the settle which at least offered some concealment.

With a muffled mutter, she pressed closer. Brock licked her lips and dared another foray into her mouth. This time, her tongue fluttered against his. That tentative welcome rushed through him like wildfire. He drew back, hoping she'd take his lead. Praise the angels, she did. As her tongue slid into his mouth, he sucked on it and she gave another hum, a longer, voluptuous note of surrender.

He'd never found innocence appealing. Too much risk of misunderstandings. His lovers were women who knew what they wanted. But teaching this widow how to kiss set his heart clenching with more tenderness. A tenderness that proved an incongruous companion to his craving to conquer and possess.

So while the kiss melted into passion, sweetness lingered. Brock had kissed more women than he cared to remember, yet he'd never experienced a kiss like this one.

By heaven, he'd remember this kiss. The day he died, he'd think back to Selina Martin's tongue in his mouth and her graceful body trembling between his hands.

Because now she caught onto the basics, she proved an infernally adept student. He hauled her across his lap to give him better access to her mouth. Plastered to him as she was, she must know the effect she had on him. His heart crashed against his ribs over and over, and his cock swelled with hungry demand as her kiss turned voracious.

She was warm, fragrant, and desperate. He usually didn't find desperation to his liking either. But Selina's wholehearted desire was the most exciting thing he'd ever known.

Too exciting. If she kept kissing him, he'd push her down onto the cushioned seat and have her. To hell with discretion. And while the wicked, selfish side of his nature would like nothing better, he'd promised to look after her.

Selina roused his rusty honor from its long sleep. Brock lifted his head, ignoring her murmur of disappointment, and stared down at her in wonder and regret. Because he'd like nothing better than to rip away that ugly dress and squeeze her breasts and cup her delectable rump and part her legs and slide deep inside her.

Soon...

When he held her in his arms like this, soon wasn't soon enough.

"We must stop," he said gruffly.

Her eyes were heavy with desire. "Yes," she said with no conviction whatsoever.

Despite his agony of frustration, a grunt of reluctant amusement escaped him. "We shouldn't have started."

Her cheeks were flushed, and her lips were full and red from his kisses. "I've wanted to kiss you since I first saw you."

As ever, her honesty carved a great rift in his heart. "Tomorrow, you can kiss me all you like."

"It seems a cursed long way off."

A pox on it, it did. It took an almighty amount of willpower to shift her off his knees and lift his hands away from her. A reminder of how close he verged to consigning any thought of scandal to perdition.

"Dream of me." He stood up and stepped back, although he had a grim foreboding that he could retreat as far as Cathay without it making a scrap of difference to his captivity.

"I do," she whispered, staring up at him with unabashed hunger.

He closed his eyes and told himself he couldn't tumble Selina Martin in Lord Derwent's library. Tonight she'd told him so much. She'd revealed even more in what she hadn't said. One selfish sod had already shared her bed, and Brock feared she went to another in a fortnight. Now she deserved a man who took time and care to coax every ounce of sensuality from that slender body.

"Selina..." he said on a groan.

"I know."

He opened his eyes to catch such longing on her face that he couldn't help surging forward.

This time, she raised a trembling hand to stop him coming closer. She stood. "Don't touch me again, or I won't go. We're not safe here."

With yearning eyes, he watched her leave. He told himself he couldn't rush after her and catch her and carry her upstairs to his room. On her way out, she didn't look back, he guessed because she teetered as close to forsaking all caution as he did.

"We'll be safe tomorrow," he said after her.

But Brock knew he lied. Because the passion that flared between him and Selina Martin was the kind that shook kingdoms. When desire burned so hot, nowhere was safe.

CHAPTER THREE

"**B**ut, madam, I can't leave you here on your own. What if your friend doesn't come for you?"

Nor far off crying with frustration, Selina stared at her maid Kitty and, God forgive her, cursed the girl's loyalty and affection. They were in a private parlor at the Blue Wagon, which was a bustling coaching inn about an hour away from the Derwent estate.

Everything this morning had gone so smoothly. It even worked to Selina's advantage that she wasn't selling her carriage and horses until just before Christmas. If she'd traveled in one of Cecil's vehicles, she'd have had much more trouble sneaking away.

Everything had gone so smoothly. Until now.

Last night, it had seemed a simple matter to say that she'd send Kitty on to London, while she remained behind to await Lord Bruard. In practice, Kitty was horrified to think of abandoning Selina alone at a public inn.

"I'm sure she'll come, Kitty," she said for what felt like the hundredth time.

"I don't mind waiting."

"But John Coachman is eager to get back to London."

"He can sit tight, too. You're too kind to your servants. We're meant to wait on your convenience, not you wait on ours."

"My friend lives nearby," she said with barely concealed desperation. "She won't be far away."

A mulish expression settled on the girl's pretty, freckled face. "Even more reason for me to wait then, Miss Selina."

She hadn't been Miss Selina since she was seventeen and a new bride, but Kitty had worked for her parents and at times of stress slipped back into her old ways.

Selina felt sick with frustration. All her life, she'd done her best to be a good woman and live by the moral principles that her parents had instilled in her. Now she had a mere week to go to the bad. Surely heaven would allow her such a small measure of selfish pleasure in a life that promised nothing but duty and decorum. Last night, she'd caught a glimpse of the glories awaiting her in Lord Bruard's arms. She wanted more. The idea that those few, admittedly spectacular kisses, might end up being her ration of joy made her want to bawl her eyes out.

"Kitty, you could take your own advice and obey me when I say I'm in no danger and I want you to leave me." She struggled to sound stern, as she never was with her maid. "This is a respectable inn."

The girl shook her head, unimpressed with Selina's attempt at authority. "It's still a public house, and you're a pretty woman without protection. Gentlemen will pester you."

Oh, how Selina wished they would. Or one particular gentleman anyway. "I can look after myself."

Kitty laughed at that. "Lord above, you're as innocent as a lamb, madam. Despite having your lovely boy and being married to that blackguard Mr. Martin for coming up on ten years."

"I've told you I won't have you criticizing the late master."

"All right, I won't – but that doesn't mean he doesn't deserve criticism. Having a kind lady like you at home and rushing around after all those hussies, I ask you."

"That's enough, Kitty," she said with such sharpness that the girl looked startled. Kitty was right about one thing. Selina was too soft on her servants. Cecil had admonished her about it often enough. "You will leave me here this very minute. I'm in no danger. I'm an adult. And I pay you to take my direction."

To her dismay, the unusually harsh tone had Kitty bursting into tears. "Oh, Miss Selina, I'm sorry I've vexed you, but you can't ask me to desert you. Not when you might run into trouble that you have no idea how to handle. It's not fair."

"Kitty..." Selina sighed with a mixture of irritation and fondness. She went up and placed her arms around the sobbing girl. "Don't take on so."

Then to make an already awkward situation worse, there was a quick knock on the door and Lord Bruard marched in with a purposeful stride that only made Selina feel guiltier than ever. "Selina, what the devil is keeping you? Oh..."

Kitty wrenched free of Selina's arms and stopped crying with a loud hiccup. "Your lordship!"

Selina ran damp palms down the front of her faded olive green traveling dress and wondered how on earth she ever imagined she'd manage this intrigue. She'd always been terrible at lying.

Whenever she infringed the rules as a girl, she was always caught.

She might yearn to go to Lord Bruard's bed. That didn't suddenly turn her into a convincing deceiver.

But this is all I'll have. This is all I'll ever have, a voice cried out inside her. *It's wrong. I know it's wrong. But a week of sin in an otherwise blameless life can't be too much to ask.*

Apparently it was.

The tears she'd been fighting sprang to her eyes, but she was too conscious of Kitty's curious stare to let them fall. Nothing could keep her voice from thickening with betraying emotion. "Lord Bruard, what a pleasant surprise to see you."

Brock was quick off the mark. She had to give him that. He put on a more formal air and bowed. "Mrs. Martin, any sign of your friend yet? I'm more than happy to drive you to your destination, if you fear she's been delayed."

To her chagrin, Kitty was no fool either. With unconcealed shock, her sharp gaze shifted from Selina to Brock then back again.

"Madam..." She'd gone as red as a beetroot. So had Selina.

"Excellent, my lord. Thank you. I'll take you up on that offer." Selina turned back to a dumbstruck Kitty. "So you see, no need to worry about me. Lord Bruard will drive me to my friend's door. You and John can go back to London now."

"He called you Selina," Kitty said in a flat tone.

"I have no manners," Brock said. "Pardon me, Mrs. Martin."

"Kitty, I'm going to spend next week with a school friend." Selina spoke slowly and with emphasis, in case the maid needed to repeat the details, should anyone inquire about her mistress's whereabouts. "Then I'm returning to London, so I'm there when Gerald comes home from school. On Boxing Day, I'm marrying Mr. Canley-Smythe. As I told you, a quiet week with a congenial companion is just what I need before what promises to be a busy time."

"I understand," Kitty said.

To Selina's mortification, she could see that the maid did indeed understand. And not the weak tale of wanting to visit some mythical school friend Kitty had never heard of. The girl could be in no doubt that the congenial companion was in fact one of London's most notorious rakes.

"A few days out of my usual routine will do me a world of good."

As Kitty's eyes rested on Selina, they were alight with compassion and far too much comprehension for comfort. She'd never confided in Kitty about her reasons for marrying Cecil. But it was clear now that her maid had long ago recognized what was at stake.

"That they will. I'm sorry to make such a fuss. I'll go back to London and if anyone asks where you are, I'll say you're visiting an old friend."

Selina sought but didn't find any trace of condemnation in the girl's bright blue eyes. "I'll be back next Wednesday."

"As you wish, madam." The girl curtsied. "My lord."

Once Kitty had left, Selina released a deep sigh of relief. "I'm sorry. I couldn't get her to go. We can trust her not to tell anyone the truth."

"I came so close to making a complete mess of everything." Brock crossed the room to take her into his arms. "I'm sorry, my darling."

The "my darling" went a long way toward soothing her ragged nerves. She sagged against him, resting her head on his shoulder. The scents of leather and horses and lemon soap, and something spicy that was him, made her head swim. It was ridiculous, but she still felt like crying. "For a moment there, I feared that I wouldn't get away. She's very protective."

"I'm glad someone is. You seem to have always been so hideously alone."

"I'm not alone now," she murmured, rising to kiss the hard line of his jaw.

His hold tightened. "No, you're not alone now."

Selina hadn't been sure how she'd feel when she ran away to give herself to a lover. She'd spent most of the night fretting over whether she could do this wicked thing. She didn't give a fig about surrendering her virtue to Brock. She'd been his from the moment she saw him. But she owed allegiance to two males, and what she did threatened them in ways she couldn't justify.

She wasn't yet wed to Cecil. If she was, however urgent her desire, she wouldn't sneak into another man's bed. But nonetheless she'd made promises to Cecil, and her presence here with Brock broke every one of them.

If anyone discovered her transgression and made it known, Gerald would be dragged into the ensuing scandal. Not to mention that she'd lose any chance to offer him a secure future.

She'd arrived at the Blue Wagon in a lather of nerves and self-recrimination, none of which made her any less determined to grab her one chance at happiness. Having to put Kitty off the scent had tested her to the limit. Then all her effort turned out to be in vain, anyway.

Now she stood in Brock's embrace and none of that mattered. What mattered was that at last she'd share her body with the man she wanted.

"I must be terrifically wicked," she murmured, half to herself.

"Not terrifically," he said with a hint of tender amusement. "Why so harsh?"

She knew that while this was a once-in-a-lifetime event for her, he didn't take their affair with anything like the same seriousness. But that was difficult to remember when he spoke as if he understood her better than anyone else in the world. "I'm about to become a fallen woman, and I've never been so happy. That makes me wicked."

"No, merely human." He pulled away far enough to stare down into her face. His expression mirrored the tenderness she heard in his voice. "I'm glad you're happy. There hasn't been enough happiness in your life."

When he smiled at her as if she was the dearest treasure in the world, Selina's heart melted into a dollop of honey. Heavens, no wonder he cut such a swathe through the ranks of the ladies. He was utterly irresistible.

Selina stopped herself there. She didn't want to think about his other lovers. The ones preceding her – or the ones to come.

She spoke with sudden fierceness. "Let's go, Brock. Let's not waste a second of the time we have. I want to feel your touch. I want you to take me. I don't want to wonder any longer. I want to know. And I want you to show me."

The anticipation that blazed in his eyes made her toes curl in her fur-lined half boots. "In that case, we'll be on our way. I think there will be snow tonight. I want us tucked up safe inside before the weather changes."

Feeling reckless and brave as she never had before, she caught his hand and turned toward the door. Ruin might lie ahead, but never did a woman rush toward her ravishment with such an eager heart. "You'll keep me warm."

"Aye, I will at that, lassie." She'd already noticed that when his feelings were engaged, traces of a beguiling Scottish brogue emerged. "But not so fast. We have some unfinished business first."

Puzzled, she turned back. "Unfinished business?"

"Aye."

Laughter lit his eyes. Laughter and desire. Another rush of excitement sizzled through her.

He tugged her back into his arms. "This."

Brock kissed her with a heated determination that made her quake. She responded with all the fervent passion burning inside her.

When he lifted his head, he looked as shaken as she felt. "My God, Selina, I have an almighty hunger for you. I hope you know what you're inviting."

She gave a throaty laugh. "I don't. That's what makes this week such an adventure."

After another brief kiss, he drew her toward the door. "Heaven is waiting for us, my darling. Let's go and find it."

CHAPTER FOUR

"*D*id you mean what you said at the inn?" Brock leaned back against the red leather seat of his luxurious coach, as it rolled through the flat Essex countryside. Outside, it was cold but clear, although senses honed during his Scottish childhood told him that there would be snow before tomorrow morning.

Tomorrow morning, when he'd wake up in his hunting box with a new and bewitching mistress in his arms.

Selina turned from looking out the window at the beautiful, if bleak landscape.

The light shone stark gray on her delicate features. It still astonished him that even with her unassuming manner, people missed how lovely she was. Of course, she dressed like a damned Quaker. If only he could keep her for more than a week. He'd show her off as she deserved to be shown off, in rich colors and extravagant fabrics. Dressed to draw attention, she'd set the world on its ear.

Steady, laddie. There's no point wishing for more than she's giving you. That way lies nothing but frustration and misery.

Nonetheless it seemed like a bloody waste that this sensual creature meant to consign herself to a blundering jackanapes like Cecil Canley-Smythe.

"What did I say?" she asked.

"That we shouldn't waste a minute."

Her answer was unhesitating. "Yes."

A slow, pleased smile stretched his lips. "We have a couple of hours before we reach the hunting box."

Her velvety brown eyes rounded, and her gloved hands clenched in her olive green skirts. Olive green! When she was born for peacock blue and crimson and emerald. The first time he saw her in her Quakerish gray gown, he'd thought of a queen disguised as a beggar maid. "You want to...begin now?"

He shrugged, although any appearance of ease was manufactured. "Not if you find the idea distasteful."

She gave a huff of self-deprecating laughter. "You must know I don't."

"I hope. But you seem so eager to sit over there on your own, I can't be sure."

She made a helpless gesture. "Are you saying you'd like me to cuddle up to you?"

"For a start."

"Forgive me. I'm such a rank beginner at this."

That damned tenderness surged again. "I suppose you've only ever done it in bed."

"Yes. Under cover of darkness. And not for years. When I realized Roderick was so...indiscriminate, I locked him out of my room."

Dear God, how she'd been shortchanged when it came to the men in her life. "Bloody fool, to seek his pleasure elsewhere when he had paradise waiting at home."

Another of those wry little exhalations of amusement. "He didn't see it like that. He said I was about as exciting as a plank of wood." She frowned. "I hope you won't feel that way."

Brock laughed, even as he wished he'd had the chance to punch the vile Roderick in the nose. "I promise I won't."

"You might need to be patient, all the same." She went back to looking troubled. "I'm not very experienced."

He gave a long-suffering sigh. "I can see that I've taken on a huge responsibility to womankind. I pray I'm up to it."

Up to it? He was half-aroused already. He reached across to pull down the blinds, plunging them into a twilit world. In the confined space, Selina's jasmine scent tinged the air with the promise of bliss.

"What do I need to do?" She sounded nervous as she crossed to sit beside him.

"Only what you feel like."

"I feel like running away back to London."

When he caught her fluttering hand, it trembled in his grip. "Do you really?"

"No." The word was a breath of sound.

Anticipation rushed through him. "Good. Will you sit on my lap?"

"Yes."

He raised his head and stared into her eyes. This close, even in the dim light, he saw flecks of green and gold in the rich brown. "First this can go."

Carefully, as though one rash move might scare her away, he untied the ribbons under her chin that held her bonnet in place. He tossed the plain straw monstrosity onto the other seat.

"Are you...are you going to undress me?"

"It's too cold." He removed his leather gloves and shoved them into his pocket, then taking his time, he slid her gloves from her slender hands. He lifted each hand to his lips, then turned them over and kissed her palms.

She made a faint sound of pleasure. How the hell had her husband failed to give her satisfaction? She was the most responsive woman he'd ever known.

Selina's unwavering stare betrayed fear and dawning excitement. He kissed her palm again, circling his tongue, relishing the taste of her skin. She shifted against the seat as arousal stirred.

"Are you ready?" he murmured.

She cast him an uncertain glance. "No."

He smiled. "Are you sure?"

The smile she gave him in return was tremulous. "No."

With a cautious movement, she reached for his shoulder. Working with the swaying carriage, she wriggled around and placed her luscious rump on his knees. The soft heat of her, so close to his cock, made him swell and harden. He released a strangled sound as his arms encircled her, holding her safe against the rocking.

"Are you all right?" she asked unsteadily.

"Aye, I'm just a little overheated."

"I'm glad. It makes me feel less at a disadvantage to know that you're on edge, too."

A grunt of amusement escaped him. "On edge? I'm a breath away from insanity."

"Is that bad?"

He bit back another groan as a bump rubbed her against him. "It is when I want to give you pleasure."

"Knowing you want me gives me pleasure."

It was his turn to be lost for words. "Selina..."

"Kiss me, Brock," she whispered, tilting her face toward his and sliding her hand along his shoulder to the nape of his neck. "I love it when you kiss me."

How could he resist? This time when he kissed her, she displayed none of last night's hesitation. She opened her mouth, and the kiss soon turned hot and voracious. By the time he pulled back, they were both panting.

With avid hands, he hauled up her skirts to reveal a froth of petticoats and long, beautiful legs. Sheer linen drawers covered her to the knees, where sky-blue garters held up white stockings.

He ran his finger around the silk ribbon. "Pretty."

Much prettier than anything else he'd seen her wear, in fact. This glimpse into a hidden sensuality was intriguing.

He glanced up at her intent face. "You keep surprising me."

She raked her fingers through his hair as if she stroked a big cat. "Nobody can see to disapprove."

"I can see, and I approve very much." He slid one hand under the loose leg of her drawers, and they both gasped when his hand met bare flesh.

He caressed her gently, venturing higher with each touch, until the linen rucked up and he cupped the damp heat of her mound. She released an audible explosion of breath, as his hand crept into her cleft and teased the heated flesh. She was slick and satiny to his touch, and when he curled his thumb over the center of her pleasure, he heard one of those hums of pleasure he loved.

He turned his head and nuzzled her soft blond hair. "May I take off your drawers?"

"Yes," she said on a long hiss, as he increased the pressure on the pearl of flesh that stiffened under his caresses.

"Thank you." He glanced a kiss across her ear and felt her shiver as his breath brushed the sensitive skin.

He was in an agony of desire, hard and aching. He'd like to rip her drawers away, but he forced his shaking hands to do their best to undo the tapes. Not since he was a raw boy had a lover made him tremble. Selina Martin possessed a magic that beggared his sophistication.

"These knots are an infernal nuisance," he grated out.

She reached down and with embarrassing ease, undid the ties. Then she wriggled some more to get the damned rag off. Brock wished he had torn her drawers away. As she shifted about on his lap, he suffered an agony of frustration and delight. After what felt like an eternity, the frail linen garment slipped to the floor.

The carriage's jolting made his torment worse – or better. Every time she connected with his aching cock, he came close to spilling. He ground his teeth and told himself he must wait, but he wanted her too much. He, the great master of sensuality, fell victim to his primitive urges.

He caught a glimpse of white thighs and a nest of light brown curls as she tortured him with more sliding and bobbing. Brock pressed back against the seat, so she had room to place her bent knees on either side of his hips. The scent of female excitement was more intoxicating than the finest French brandy.

"Like this?" she asked.

"Aye. And hold onto my shoulders."

Brock reached down, his knuckles skimming her glistening pubic hair, and ripped at the buttons on his breeches. He was in a frenzy to plunge inside her.

His dick sprang free and over the pounding of his heart, he heard her gasp. "You're so much bigger than…"

Than her late husband. "Touch me."

"It's permitted?"

Her uncertainty made him smile. "It's required."

She gave a shaky giggle. Then shock shuddered through him as she released his shoulder and reached down to curl an unsteady hand around him.

He suffered her clumsy caresses until stars exploded in his head. "Selina…stop now," he growled, catching her hand and pulling it away.

Wide brown eyes met his. "You don't like me touching you?"

"I like it too much." Hands rough with urgency, he caught her hips. "Take me."

He'd expected her to balk when the moment came, but she showed no reluctance. She gripped his shoulders and after some heart-stopping wiggling, she positioned herself over him at last.

With a voluptuous sigh of pleasure that would echo in his dreams, she sank over him. He closed his eyes as he basked in the tight, wet grip. He was a large man, but she took all of him.

For one reverberant moment, she sagged into his body and he felt her trembling reaction. Then she straightened and shifted upward. Another long glide of sexual pleasure. His balls tightened, and he was already teetering on the brink.

"Hell and damnation," he growled as she descended again. Lightning raged behind his eyes, but somehow he remembered that he'd promised to save her from getting with child.

"Selina, don't take me inside you after this," he said on a gust of breath. He suffered another glide of her body, then twisted, until her back hit the leather seat. "Hold your skirts up."

With shaking hands, she obeyed. He kneeled over her, one hand gripping the back of the seat to keep his balance. With his other hand, he grabbed his dick, as his heart crashed into his ribs with dizzying force. He pressed down, his cock pumping onto her bare stomach. The sway of the carriage added another rich note to the glorious release.

A glorious release that he was mortified to acknowledge was a one-sided event.

Brock sat up and swore, running an unsteady hand through his hair. "I'm sorry, my darling."

He wanted to tell her that this had never happened to him before, but it sounded too much like a lying excuse.

Flushed, ruffled, beautiful, she sprawled half-sitting against the side of the carriage. Her gaze was dark and confused as she stared at him. His seed shone wet on her stomach. He dug in his pocket for his handkerchief and began to clean her up.

"You want me that much?" she asked in a husky voice, as she lay still beneath his ministrations.

"Aye," he said, crumpling the square of white linen and shoving it back in his pocket. "Can you forgive me?"

To his surprise, a delighted smile curved her lips. "That you want me beyond reason? Yes, I think I might find it in my heart to forgive you."

Shocked, he stared at her. "You're damned tolerant."

Selina sat up and touched his cheek. The small gesture of comfort eased his raging self-disgust, and he believed she really did forgive him. As she smoothed her skirts, she afforded him another view of those spectacular legs. "You can do better next time."

He gave a rueful laugh. "I can. I will."

Brock studied her. Her bodice remained buttoned to the neck, all demure modesty. His hands curled into fists on his lap, as the need to see her breasts surged through him. When he got her into bed, he'd keep her there and climaxing until today's disappointment became a dim memory.

In fact, why wait for the hunting lodge? "Right now," he said.

"Now?" She waved a hand toward where his prick spilled from his open breeches. "Don't you need time to…"

"There's more than one way to skin a cat, sweetheart."

To his surprise, sensible, proper Mrs. Martin burst into a fit of enchanting giggles.

Selina gained control of her amusement in time to watch her devilish lover tuck himself back into his breeches with a leisurely lack of self-consciousness. Brock was built on impressive lines. She'd known he would be.

When she'd taken him inside her body, she felt like he filled every lonely space in her heart and soul. The effect had been extraordinary. He stretched her more than Roderick ever had, and in a way she couldn't explain, that powerful claiming had reached beyond the physical realm. Even with the disappointing finish, Brock's possession offered an emotional sustenance she'd never known before.

She knew that he was piqued at losing himself before she found her pleasure. But even that was appealing. Roderick had never cared. Early in their marriage, she'd retained the vague hope that the conjugal act might offer more than a brief and messy penetration. But her husband had been quick to inform her that no wife of his would act the whore. She'd often wondered if Roderick expected his doxies to lie like a log while he grunted and heaved over them.

How would Cecil use her body? Would he show as little genuine interest in her as Roderick had? Some deep feminine instinct warned her that he wanted more than occasional compliance. She hid a shudder at the thought.

"What's wrong?"

She wasn't used to a man – to anyone – paying attention to her. "Nothing."

Brock was frowning. "You went from laughing to looking like you contemplated your own hanging."

He wasn't far wrong. Sometimes she felt like her approaching marriage wasn't much of an improvement over an execution. But Selina refused to let grim thoughts intrude on this short affair. She had the rest of her life to come to terms with an incompatible husband. "I let my thoughts stray where they shouldn't."

Brock ran his hand through his hair. "You must be cursing me as a damned impetuous boy, but I really can do better. It's just that you make me so wild with wanting you. I'm never a greedy lover – but I'm greedy for you. Have you ever had a man's mouth on your quim?"

"Your mouth?" she stammered, carnal images invading her mind. Her womb clenched as if he already kissed her...down there.

His lips curled in a wolfish smile that made her shiver with anticipation. "Let me make up for my sins against you."

In such a way? She couldn't imagine it. But his kisses and hands had already stirred her desire to a hectic pitch. When he lost himself on her stomach, she'd barely retreated from the brink. She still wanted a climax.

When his control shattered, he'd awoken a vast tenderness. Brock always seemed a superhuman figure, above the frailties of mere mortals. Knowing that she could destroy the rake's restraint made her marvel. And preen.

So she found the courage to accept what was about to happen. "What would you like me to do?"

"Sit back and accept the pleasure." The smile intensified. "It's the least I owe you."

"Should I stay where I am?"

When he considered her with such concentration, her yearning flowered until she trembled. He spoke in a deliberate, thoughtful voice. "Easiest, I think, and no doubt safer, if you balance on the edge of the bench and spread your legs. I'll kneel in front of you."

Without hesitation, she wriggled around to place her feet flat on the floor of the bumping carriage. She was sinfully conscious that beneath her skirts, she was bare.

Her heart pounded with anticipation as she watched Brock settle on his knees before her. Anticipation and nerves. She'd never considered this as a sensual variation. It seemed bizarre. Bizarre, but breathtakingly exciting. She was mere hours into her descent to ruin. She'd ridden on a man's lap, and now her lover's mouth would explore her sex.

Gently Brock pushed up her skirts to reveal her thighs and stomach. A stomach that felt tight and heavy with burgeoning arousal. When he bent to kiss her thighs, the heat of his lips shuddered through her like an explosion. She stared down at his thick dark hair, disheveled after she'd run her hands through it when he thrust inside her.

"Hold your skirts up for me," he murmured.

Selina fumbled to obey as he pushed her knees apart, his eyes glued to the secret hollows of her body. She told herself that once she'd accepted Brock's invitation to become his lover, modesty had no place. But she couldn't silence twenty-seven years of virtue so easily. Right now, she was frantic to cover herself.

"I'm making you nervous," he said without looking up.

More of that perception. Again it surprised her.

"Yes," she admitted.

"You'll like this."

"I'm sure I will. But you're staring."

"That's because you're so damned beautiful."

She'd been blushing since he'd suggested kissing her...there. Now her cheeks went as hot as fire. "I can't imagine..."

"Believe me, you're beautiful. Everywhere." As if to prove he meant it, he leaned in so close, she felt a humid puff of breath on her mound. The sensation summoned a deep liquid response from inside her that left her gasping.

Brock growled with approval. "Lean back and tilt your hips forward."

Selina obeyed, reaching to hook one trembling hand through the strap dangling from the roof. She tried not to think how this new position exposed her even more blatantly. As the vehicle bounced along the rough road, she caught her breath and held it.

Every muscle tightened while she braced for his mouth to touch her cleft. Instead he began to kiss her thighs, nipping, licking, tasting. On an audible gust, she exhaled. With possessive caresses that made her quiver like a sapling in a gale, his hands ran up and down her legs.

Only when she was shivering with need did he spread her legs wider and place his mouth over her center. Fire raged through her, threatened to incinerate her to smoking ash.

"Brock!" she cried out, bucking up toward him and releasing her creased skirts to grab his hair.

When his tongue started to explore every intimate fold, shock held her motionless. Then he found the place that turned her to quaking jelly. He teased her until pleasure swelled in a great wave. She'd been reaching for her peak before he pulled out of her. This time, the crest of sensation flung her higher and higher.

Selina cried out again in joy and gratitude as a spasm of rapture cramped every muscle. When she returned to the world, he remained kneeling between her legs. His green eyes were heavy with satisfaction, although he'd done nothing to take care of his own release.

"That was...wonderful." Her voice was thick with the lingering effects of her climax. She untangled her hand from the strap. At the height, she'd clutched it so hard that the leather had bitten into her palm. Astonishment made her stammer. "I had no idea."

Brock bent his head to place a kiss on her curls and shifted back. Through dazed eyes, she watched him wipe his mouth. Something about his ease with what they'd done banished her excruciating embarrassment. "Shall we try the other again?"

She felt like she'd been racked upon the stars. She felt like her bones had dissolved into hot syrup. "I doubt I could sit up."

"I'll hold onto you." He regarded her with steady interest that summoned another blush. "The decision is yours."

When she'd surrendered to that searing release, she'd assumed that she'd feel sated, at least until they reached the hunting lodge. Now staring into his intent dark face, fresh restlessness stirred.

Because when his big body united with hers, she'd felt whole for the first time in her life. It was dangerous to lend an emotional slant to what she and Brock did. She'd find it difficult enough to reconcile herself to a future without sensual satisfaction, especially after what she'd just discovered. Only a fool would talk herself into a broken heart as well. But even knowing the risk, something in her soul had yearned toward him when they joined.

And she'd wanted more.

"In that case, I'm all yours."

He rose to resume his place on the seat. This time, she kept her balance better and her movements were less awkward as she placed herself over him.

Nor was he in such a furious hurry, although the bulge in his breeches betrayed his fierce need. Instead of opening his front fall and pulling her down onto him, he began to kiss her with languid pleasure, as if time had no meaning.

Selina let him draw her into a game of lips and tongues and teeth. While she treated this affair as deadly serious, she found herself ready to tease, too. Nipping at his lips. Dipping her tongue into his mouth. Advancing and pulling back in a flirtatious dance.

His hands roamed up and down her back, tracing her spine, shaping her hips and descending to cup her buttocks and crush her into his hardness. She gasped as she felt the pressure of his erection. He hadn't yet caressed her breasts, already heavy and aching for his touch.

She started her own exploration of his body and cursed the barriers of clothing, although she kept enough grip on reality to know that they couldn't go naked in a coach on the King's highway. But through the black superfine of his coat, she discovered the sinewy muscles of his shoulders and arms and the hard expanse of his chest and back.

Brock kissed her as if he couldn't get enough of the taste of her mouth. She'd never kissed anyone like this in her life. Roderick hadn't seen the point in kissing. This revelation of the pleasure that lips could conjure charmed and beguiled her. And compelled her to the edge of desire.

Selina was the one who lost patience with this seductive game. She crammed closer and tried to extend each kiss beyond playful enjoyment to passion. When he kept up the teasing, she growled in frustration. She'd been tunneling her hand through his hair. Now she tugged hard and held his head as she stared into his glittering eyes.

"You're driving me mad, plague take you."

He was panting, and a flush marked his slanted cheekbones. His lips might tease, but his heavy gaze told her that he rapidly moved past kisses, too.

"So what are you going to do about it?"

She realized then that while he might make allowances for her inexperience, he expected her to play the full partner in this seduction. "You want me to take the lead?" she asked, her voice shaky with a resurgence of nerves.

"If that appeals to you."

For a bleak moment, Roderick's scathing response to her attempts to please him echoed in her ears. Then she dismissed the memory. Brock wasn't Roderick. Brock had given her more delight in the last two hours than Roderick had given her in nine years together.

"Tell me if I do anything wrong."

"Do what you like, and you won't go wrong."

"I don't know what I like." She paused, cheeks heating. "Well, I like it when you're inside me. And I like it when you touch me...down there."

His smile conveyed the tenderness that cut straight through to her heart like a knife through butter. "That's a start."

She paused. "And I like kissing you."

Selina suited her actions to her words and dragged his head forward until their lips met once more. This time there was no teasing. Naked passion flared, and the desire coiling in her stomach expanded into a sharp ache.

When she shifted on his knees in an instinctive attempt to find some surcease from that throbbing, needy emptiness, he groaned against her lips. The hands holding her hips tightened to the edge of bruising. She waited in an agony of suspense for him to take it further, until she recalled that what happened next was up to her.

Selina retreated far enough away to suck in a breath tinged with the musky scent of arousal. Hers as well as his. The smell of his skin had taunted her since last night, when he'd made his wicked proposition. Now that heated male essence set her senses on fire.

She wanted Brock to plunge into her. She wanted him to fill her, until every barrier between them dissolved. She wanted to reach a climax while a man she desired was inside her.

Her vision was blurry with need when she released the shoulder she clutched so frantically. "Hold onto me."

"Always."

Even in her urgency, she knew that was just lovers' talk, not to be trusted. But she trusted the firmness of his grip enough to reach down with both hands and fumble with the buttons of his breeches.

"You're killing me," he ground out, bucking his hips up.

She had the giddy feeling that she might tumble to the floor. Biting her lip, she struggled to concentrate through the blood pounding in her ears. "I've never undressed a man before. Be patient."

At last, she found the trick of it. Not that the fastenings were complicated. But clarity of thought was impossible when she was in such a fever.

They both heaved a sigh of relief when his rod rose from his open breeches. She curled a shaking hand around him, marveling at the heat and power in her grip. He groaned again and closed his eyes as if he were in pain.

"Am I hurting you?" Selina asked, despite his earlier assurances.

"I'm dying," he muttered, then opened eyes that gleamed with wicked humor. "For want of you."

She stifled a giggle and squeezed, until strain tightened his striking features. "You'll have to teach me how to touch you."

Humor twisted his mouth. "You're doing a fine job on your own."

Gripping more tightly, she slid her hand up and down, feeling the hard veins pulsing under the silky skin. His organ fascinated her. It seemed a privilege to discover Brock's nakedness.

With his wife, Roderick had been a modest man, although she couldn't imagine he was half so shy with his whores. All she'd known of her husband's genitals was as a hard and painful presence shoving into her.

In gratitude, she kissed Brock. His unabashed desire set off another of those hot surges of craving. She shifted until she clasped him tight between her spread legs. Moving with the carriage, she descended to take him with remarkable ease. It was as if she'd been created to fit him.

"Selina..." he said on a long drawn-out hiss of pleasure, as his hands flexed on her hips under the fall of her skirts. He looked eager and hungry, but she caught the ghost of something more profound in his eyes.

The vehicle's sway shifted her over him in a most arousing way. She'd never thought of enjoying a lover's touch in a speeding vehicle. The experience proved...piquant.

Cautiously she rose, drawing a long, guttural groan from him. His grasp tightened as she lowered. She curled her hands over his shoulders, although she knew he wouldn't let her fall.

"Use me," he said in a gravelly voice.

"I will." She hardly noted what she said. She was too aware of the hard, throbbing flesh filling her. Pleasure spiraled as she settled into a rhythm that matched the carriage's lurching and her own impulses. She gasped for air as her movements grew faster, uncoordinated, desperate.

The need for release coiled tighter and tighter, as the sweet friction of their union pushed her toward the edge. Brock tilted his hips and went deeper.

"Let me," he said.

"Yes." She cried out as he reached beneath her skirts to find her sex. The world dissolved into cascading stars. Hurtling through an agony of delight, she clenched hard around him.

Brock caught her up for a carnal, openmouthed kiss before he lifted her off him. She lay back, struggling to keep her place on the seat as the coach swayed.

He fumbled for his handkerchief and spilled into it. When he'd finished, he released a quivering sigh and collapsed against the red leather upholstery.

Tremors of bliss still shook Selina. She'd just soared to heights of rapture that she'd never imagined existed. "You're a considerate lover."

"I promised." Weariness weighted his answer, as he leaned his head back and closed his eyes.

He took care of her, as he vowed he would. It was rank stupidity to feel cheated at the waste of his seed outside her body. Yet cheated she felt. She wanted him so much. Part of that wanting was for him to give her everything.

"Is it satisfying to pull out like that?"

Without opening his eyes, he raised expressive black eyebrows. "I find it preferable to using a sheath."

"What's a sheath?"

A hint of fondness softened his smile. "You're such a damned fascinating mixture, Selina. You take me to heaven and back by riding me like you were born to service me. It makes me forget how innocent you are."

"I'm unworldly," she said with a hint of grimness, sitting up gingerly and sliding her feet to the floor. "Not innocent. There's a difference."

This time, he focused those acute green eyes on her. "Aye, you're right. Nobody who has been through what you have could be called untouched."

"So what's a sheath?"

"Sewn sheep gut that covers the cock and stops the seed reaching the woman."

"Ugh!" she said with a grimace. "Doesn't it slip off at the height of..."

His grunt expressed amusement. "You tie it on with ribbons."

She couldn't contain a giggle. "Good Lord."

"Aye, it's quite a sight."

Selina stared down to where his organ lay flaccid. Even now, it was impressive. Brock must have noted her concentrated attention, because his rod twitched and began to harden.

She'd have thought the prospect of further congress would hold no immediate appeal after that last volcanic encounter, but even so, a spark stirred. She loved having him inside her. The degree of intimacy in their joining had astonished her. Whenever Roderick had used her, she just felt lonely and awkward. After what she'd just shared with her wicked lover, she felt like a goddess.

Brock fastened his breeches and pulled his watch from his pocket. "Later. We're too close to the hunting lodge."

She blushed, which was absurd given she'd just passed the most abandoned hours of her life. "You're turning me into a libertine."

He smiled at her with a lazy appreciation that only bolstered her sensual interest. "I do hope so, lassie."

Still blushing, feeling ridiculously shy, she bent to pick up her drawers then wondered what to do with them.

"Put them on," he murmured. "I want to watch you."

"Brock..."

His smile intensified. "It would give me untold pleasure to see you cover up the places that I have plans to uncover again as soon as I can."

"Very well," she said, but her hands were unsteady as she wriggled back into her drawers. Brock had to help her with the tapes. The brush of his fingers on her bare skin set off little explosions of arousal inside her. He seemed to find the experience just as titillating.

By the time he finished, they were both breathing in uneven gasps. He rested one elegant hand on her mound then released her.

"Will you help to make me decent?" she asked. "I must look like you've dragged me through a hedge."

His eyes appraised her with more of that unfettered approval. He could have no idea the potent effect that expression had on her. Both Roderick and Cecil viewed her as a project that required constant improvement. Whereas Brock acted as if he beheld an unparalleled masterpiece.

"I have no interest in making you decent, my darling." Another of those secret smiles. "Not when I've just discovered how ravishing you are when you choose to be *indecent*."

Selina laughed, knowing she should feel guilty or self-conscious, instead of giddy and elated. After all, she'd just been thoroughly debauched by a man to whom she wasn't married.

In the middle of the day. In a carriage.

The angels must weep for her. But while heaven might abhor her fall, she was a mere mortal and she'd never felt so happy.

"Well, at least help me with my bonnet."

With amusement narrowing his eyes, Brock was so handsome that her heart performed somersaults. "Why didn't you say so?"

CHAPTER FIVE

he short December day drew to a close when Brock's carriage pulled up outside a neat two-story house in gray stone in the middle of a salt marsh. Selina stared with dazed eyes across the flat, rather desolate landscape. She assumed the continuous thunder in the distance was the sea.

Brock leaned across to unlatch the door. "I promised you privacy for our week."

"I see you've delivered."

He stepped out and extended his hand. She stumbled on the step as the freezing salt-tinged air struck her like a blow. After all they'd done in the carriage, long-unused muscles protested when she moved. Her grip on his hand tightened, as she feared her knees mightn't keep her upright.

"Hold tight." He swung her up into his arms.

She'd felt dizzy leaving the carriage. She felt even dizzier now. Brock's delicious scent enveloped her, along with a radiant heat. It was bitterly cold. She wasn't surprised to feel a few soft flakes of snow brush her nose.

The door to the house opened, and a middle-aged man and woman bustled down the steps toward them.

"My lord, welcome, welcome." The man had a thick Scottish accent, much more noticeable than Brock's attractive lilt. "And tae the lady also."

Selina stiffened in Brock's arms. Cringing with embarrassment, she buried her face in his shoulder. She hadn't expected the house to be staffed. Although common sense said that it must be. She supposed the coachman must know why she and his master sought out this isolated place, but the idea of a host of people witnessing her fall from grace made her flinch.

"Jock and Mary, how good to see you after all this time. Let me get Mrs. Martin inside out of the cold."

Selina muffled a protest at the use of her real name. "It's all right," Brock murmured, as he strode up the shallow flight of steps leading to the open door. He paused at the top to turn back to the coachman. "Thank you, Erskine. I'll wager you're looking forward to a warm fire and a good meal, too."

"Aye, my lord. It's going to be a braw cold night." The coachman sounded as Scottish as Jock and Mary. "The horses made good time."

"Aye, they've earned their oats. Well done, laddie."

"Come away in, my lord," Mary said with a wide smile. Jock was busy lifting the bags from the back of the coach. "I've got fires going in the bedroom and the drawing room, and a good hot dinner on the way for ye. With all that traveling, ye both must be tired and half-starved. We got your letter, and all is as ye asked."

"Excellent. I knew I could rely on you, Mary."

Her cheeks on fire, Selina barely dared to glance up as they entered the modest hall. Behind them, she heard the coach trundle away. She assumed there were stables and other outbuildings behind the house.

"I can walk," she muttered into Brock's coat, as it became clear he intended to carry her all the way upstairs.

His hold firming, he started to mount the steps. "I like to carry you."

She liked it, too, although the act held a disturbingly bridal air. It was as if the earl brought a new and cherished wife to the house, instead of a woman he used for his pleasure over the space of a week.

"I'll bring up the hot water, my lord," Mary said from below. Jock carried the bags inside and placed them on the black and white tiled floor, before he closed the door behind him.

"Thank you," Brock said without stopping.

Having made her token bid for independence, Selina subsided into his arms. She wasn't going to object to any chance to be close to him.

Brock swept her into a large room decorated in a masculine style, all dark wood paneling and massive oak furniture. Large windows looked out over a darkening world, although light gleamed on a distant line of silver that Selina realized must be the sea. With a gentleness that touched her heart, he set her on her feet in front of the blazing fire. The warmth was welcome after the cold outside.

"You didn't expect to see the staff," he said, stepping back.

"No, although I should have realized you had people to look after the house. Was it wise to use my real name?"

"They're my kinfolk. They offer their chieftain a loyalty beyond that of mere servants. They'll go to the grave without a whisper of your visit."

Selina sighed. She'd felt so happy and daring and free in the carriage. Now she felt like a temporary mistress. Shabby and disposable. The intrusion of other people into her sensual idyll made her too aware of how the world would view her actions, if word ever got out. "I suppose they're used to you turning up with various women."

He sent her an unreadable look. "I've never brought another woman here. Jock and Mary will treat you with every respect. They know that I use this house as a refuge. If I've invited a lover to share it, she must be a lady of more than usual significance."

She shouldn't feel special when he said that. "More than usual significance" didn't count as a declaration of eternal fealty. Even if she was looking for declarations of eternal fealty.

"I'm being silly," she said. "I'm not used to being a fallen woman."

"Stop saying that." His hand cut through the air and indicated his displeasure. "You give yourself to me for desire's sake. I give myself to you for the same reason. The world's shallow judgments have no power over what we do while we're here."

The world's shallow judgments would destroy her, should her surrender become public. Selina kept that unpalatable thought to herself. She'd committed to this path. It was too late for second thoughts, even if she wanted to have them. She had a mere week to enjoy Brock's touch. Once she left this house, she'd have a lifetime to wallow in guilt and regret.

"Kiss me, Brock." She held out her hand, dismayed to see how it shook. "When you take me in your arms, it's easy to feel brave."

Approval glowed in his smile. "That's the spirit."

He drew her into the shelter of his body for a long kiss, redolent with sweetness rather than passion. Selina melted into helpless response. She loved it when he kissed her as if he'd die for lack of having her. But the strange truth was that when he kissed her like this, the effect on her susceptible heart was more powerful than when he kissed her as if he wanted to devour her.

His embrace made her feel so safe that she didn't step away when Mary came in with two steaming ewers of hot water, followed by Jock with the bags.

Mary set one jug on the mahogany washstand in the corner and carried the other through to what Selina assumed was the dressing room next door.

"Shall I unpack for ye, my lord, madam?" Mary asked when she came back into the bedroom.

"Aye, please," Brock said, moving away from Selina. "By the way, I didn't introduce you all downstairs. Mrs. Martin, these are my kinfolk Mary and Jock Drummond. They take very good care of this house while I'm away."

Mary curtsied. "Madam, we hope ye enjoy your stay. We'll do our best to make this a happy visit."

"Thank you," Selina said. "It's a beautiful place."

Jock bowed. "Aye, it's nae bad. But it's nae the Highlands." He was smiling as he carried Brock's bag through to the dressing room.

Mary lifted Selina's bag onto the bed and started to lay out its contents on the gold and blue brocade cover. "Have ye been to Scotland, madam?"

"No, I haven't."

The servants' informal air contrasted with Derwent Hall, where the staff were trained to speak only when spoken to. This ease made Selina feel more relaxed.

"Och, that's a great pity. It's a bonny country."

"I'm sure." She'd always wanted to travel, but while Roderick would go as far as Timbuctoo for a horse race or a boxing match, he'd never have contemplated taking his wife with him. Cecil made regular visits to his mills in the north. She supposed that after she married him, she'd accompany him on occasion.

Brock took her hand and drew her toward a wide window seat. Outside, the darkness deepened. This house was so isolated, no lights shone across the endless marshes spreading around them. "You'd love Bruard," he said softly.

Feeling more at home by the minute, she left her hand in his. Mary displayed no salacious curiosity about her master's relations with his new mistress. "Tell me about your home."

"It's a castle in the far north, a day's ride from the sea. It was built at the height of the age of chivalry and has four strong towers. Bruard has never been taken in war, although plenty have tried. You could walk a day in any direction without leaving Drummond lands."

Images of knights and damsels and moated fortresses flooded her mind. "It sounds like something from a fairy story."

"The castle stands above a loch, and on a calm day, the reflection is perfect. Not that we have so many calm days in the Highlands, mind you. The high hills surround it in green, except in summer, when the braes turn purple with heather. A river runs through the glen, teeming with trout and salmon."

Selina watched Brock's face as he spoke. She couldn't mistake how much he loved his home. "It must be glorious."

"Aye, that it is." She noticed that here with his kinfolk, the Scots tinge in his voice became more noticeable. This glimpse into the man beneath the rakish veneer thrilled her. She found the rake irresistible, but the man who spoke of his home with such longing threatened to steal her heart away.

His hold firmed on her hand. "I wish I could take you there."

"So do I," she admitted, although that wasn't the entire truth.

Oh, she'd dearly love to see the landscape he described. But she couldn't present herself to his clan as his mistress. It was bad enough having Mary, Jock and Erskine knowing what she was to the earl.

She regarded Brock with a faint frown. "What I don't understand is why if you love it so much, you spend most of your time down here in England."

He spread her fingers over his thigh and began to play with them. The contact was casual, yet she felt the now familiar stirring of sexual interest.

His sigh contained genuine regret. "When I was a lad, London was like a bright, shiny toy, glittering with fun and novelty."

"And women," she murmured. As if he drew her the way the moon drew the tides, she leaned in closer. Close enough for his tangy scent to become the air that she breathed.

Self-derisive humor quirked his lips. "Aye, and women, too." He paused and raised her fingers to his lips. The brief kiss sent heat swirling through her blood. "But lately, I find myself missing Scotland. A man can think in the hills in a way that he can't amid the hurly-burly of Town. Five years ago, I doubt I'd have valued the chance to think. But now..."

"Now the wild whirl has lost its charm."

He glanced at her with an almost diffident expression. "Playing the devilish Lord Bruard becomes wearisome, although don't mistake me, the devilish Lord Bruard has had a devil of a good time."

She stared down at their joined hands and spoke in a wistful tone. "Our lives have been so different. You've done just as you like, and I've never had the chance to follow my inclinations. Even when I became a widow, I couldn't forget that I had to make a secure home for Gerald."

On the far side of the room, Mary had finished unpacking Selina's valise. Now she went through to the dressing room. Selina's low-voiced conversation with Brock would have been only a murmur to her, and they hadn't broached on particularly personal subjects. Yet Selina felt her tension ease, now that they were alone.

Mary and Jock must know that she was here to share Brock's bed. There wasn't even a hint that they'd prepared a separate chamber for him. Yet to her relief, Selina noticed no judgment in their manner.

Displeasure deepened Brock's voice. "I can't stomach the thought of a woman as magnificent as you tied to that prosy bore. He'll order you around without mercy, you know. And he's completely under his mother's thumb."

A bleak smile turned Selina's lips down, although amusement was the last thing she felt. "His mother doesn't like me."

"Why would she? She's jealous, and she doesn't want another woman taking up her son's attention." His voice developed a somber note. "You're lining up for an unhappy future, my darling."

She loved it when he called her his darling, although the cynic inside her recognized that he'd had darlings before and he'd have darlings again. But that knowledge didn't stop her heart leaping with pleasure when he spoke the words. He sounded like he meant them, as if he genuinely cared for her.

"I have a son to worry about. My happiness isn't important."

He looked unimpressed. "Is there really no alternative? No economies you can make, nobody you can ask for help?"

She shook her head. "I've considered every alternative. I can scrape together funds to leave London and live somewhere quietly, but I can't afford Gerald's school fees, and he deserves better than genteel poverty. His grandmother, Roderick's mother, has offered to take him, but she's always been afraid of her own shadow. She'd remove him from school and wrap him up in flannel and liniment and keep him all to herself. He's a clever, active boy. He'd hate that. She doesn't approve of me either, so she'd do her best to keep us apart."

Brock spoke as if he weighed every word. "I could help."

Horrified, she wrenched free and surged to her feet. She felt sick with humiliation. "Oh, no, you think I'm trying to wangle money out of you."

He raised his eyes and responded calmly. "No, I don't."

"Then why would you make such an offer?"

Rueful amusement lightened his intense features. "Because I hate to see you struggle. Because the idea of you in Cecil's bed makes me want to smash something. Because I'm a rich man, and I wouldn't miss the pittance that would make all the difference to you."

Her cheeks hot, she backed away until she bumped into the huge bed that dominated the room. Bitterness soured her tone. "In effect, you'll pay for my favors as long as you enjoy them. I gather that's how these arrangements work. If I take money for what I'm willing to give you freely, you know what I become."

Chagrin tightened his features. "I've insulted you."

She folded her arms over her bosom. "Yes, you have."

"I'm sorry. That wasn't my intention." He inclined his head in what was almost a bow of apology. "Common sense says that if you can find a more congenial way to ensure your boy's future than marrying Cecil, you should take it."

"You know what the world calls women who sleep with men for money."

"I know the world is full of cruel definitions that bear little resemblance to the subtle reality of human relations."

Stubbornly, she shook her head. "I can't accept what you offer."

"Why the devil not?" He spread his hands in bewilderment. "I already know a week of you won't go near to slaking my appetite. I've never wanted a woman as much as I want you."

That insidious warmth, the same warmth she felt when he called her his darling, snaked down to form an uncomfortable mixture with her outrage. And her regret. Because without Gerald to worry about, the idea of lingering in Brock's arms was too tempting.

Lingering in his arms until he tires of you, a nasty voice said inside her head. *What happens when he moves on to the next woman who takes his fancy?*

Selina knew what would happen. He'd leave her behind with a broken heart and a ruined reputation.

"How would we manage it? Would you set me up in a discreet house somewhere? Visit me when you're free?"

"Why not?"

"And what would I tell Gerald? What happens when people find out? How will it be for him, when his school friends learn that his mother is the Earl of Bruard's doxy?"

Brock's lips tightened. "People wouldn't find out."

Her shoulders slumped with the despair that she'd spent months struggling to beat back. "People always find out," she said flatly.

"Then walk away from me after this week, but let me settle some money on you, so you can tell Cecil and his harridan of a mother to go to Hades. Accept my help, Selina, no strings attached. Don't make me have to think of you in Cecil Canley-Smythe's bed. Don't make me have to picture him heaving about all over you, grunting and sweating and touching you with those thick fingers."

She flinched at the horrid pictures Brock summoned, although he said nothing she hadn't thought herself. Unsteady hands twined in her creased olive green skirts. "You're too generous, but I can't take your money."

Self-mockery darkened his face. "Any amount of money is worth it, if it buys my peace of mind."

She shook her head. "No, you can't make me believe that you make this offer out of selfishness. You're being kind."

"I'm more than willing for you to pay me back in passion, if you feel you owe me anything."

He was joking. Selina knew he was. But her voice was adamant when she replied. "I can't accept your money, Brock. You must see that."

"I don't," he said with a hint of sulky charm. "My money saves you from Cecil. It saves me from thinking of you with Cecil."

She shook her head again, although some craven, venal part of her said she was already his lover. What would it matter if she accepted payment? The world wouldn't judge her any more kindly, if she gained no financial benefit in return for forsaking her good name. In fact, the world would no doubt call her stupid as well as loose, if she walked away with no reward for sleeping with Brock.

But Selina knew better. She made a helpless gesture, as she struggled to find the words to explain her refusal. "Last night when I accepted your invitation, I expected pleasure."

"I hope so."

"And guilt. And self-hatred. But it hasn't been like that. When you're...inside me, I feel purer than I ever have in my life. Despite the wickedness of what we do together, with you I'm true to myself in a way I've never been before."

An arrested expression settled on his striking features. "You're saying there's virtue in the honesty between us?"

"I'm saying that I vowed to love Roderick, yet I never did. I vowed that I'd be one flesh with him, yet for the last five years of our life together, I banned him from my bed."

"He was faithless."

"He was. But then, in my heart, so was I." She paused. "My contract with Cecil is based on monetary gain. He knows it. He even likes it, because his wealth gives him power over me. But the bargain between us is at base a sordid exchange. I'm selling him my body, just as much as I'd sell you my body if you paid me. The cleanest union I've entered into is this one with you. I'm here because I want you. In this house, we're equals, no matter the gulf in wealth and status between us. As you said before, we return desire for desire." She paused. "Do you understand?"

His gaze was steady and full of that admiration that bolstered her soul – and frightened her at the same time, because it would be so easy to become addicted to it. Once she left this house, she went back to being Cecil's penniless bride and meek doormat. *Yes, Cecil.*

"You're so brave. You humble me."

"Not at all."

She saw he wanted to argue, but Mary's reappearance saved her from continuing this awkward conversation. "Shall I serve dinner in an hour, my lord?"

"Does that suit you, Selina?" Brock asked.

She appreciated him checking her preferences. Cecil never did.

Oh, dear, she'd better break this habit of comparing Brock to Cecil. Cecil was her future, and if she stewed on how poorly he measured up to Lord Bruard, she invited nothing but misery. "Yes, thank you."

"I'll leave you to wash and change, then," Brock said, as Mary curtsied and left.

This had been such a disturbing day, crammed with overwhelming emotions. Selina welcomed the chance to gather her thoughts away from that perceptive green gaze. "Thank you."

But when he went through to the dressing room and shut the door behind him, all she knew was that she'd almost used up a day of her week. She didn't want to be parted from Brock for a minute of what was left.

CHAPTER SIX

 rock studied Selina over the ruins of the extravagant meal Mary had prepared for them. The flickering candlelight turned his new lover into a symphony of gold and shadows. Desire stirred, lazy now, but apt to flare into a blaze at the first encouragement.

After what they'd done in the carriage, he was surprised that he was already so eager for more. But Selina Martin had exerted this power over him, right from the first moment he saw her, so unsure and out of place amongst the Derwents' aristocratic guests. He'd wondered if his fascination might fade, once he'd had her. He never seduced unworldly women, and he'd feared the novelty of the experience might explain his obsession with her.

But having had her, he wanted her again. Having had her twice, he wanted her over and over. He already knew a mere week wouldn't quench his mighty thirst for her.

It might be futile to regret that she refused to throw Cecil over and become his mistress, but futility didn't blunt the sharpness of the pang Brock felt. He was greedy to want more than she offered, although he didn't know how to stop. Already her scent was the promise of paradise and her voice the music of the spheres.

A week was all he had.

So when he asked his question, he hoped she had other ideas. He certainly did. "Would you like to move into the drawing room for port? We can play cards, or there's a pianoforte, if you'd like a little music."

She toyed with the stem of her empty wineglass. The firelight lent amber tints to her hair, gathered up in a tumble of curls. He itched to bury his hands in that silky mass.

This evening, she wore the most elaborate of her gowns – or at least the most elaborate one he'd seen. It was still rather plain, certainly in terms of the Derwents and their milieu. But the sky-blue color made her skin look like warm cream and the bodice, while modest, hinted at the rich curves beneath.

He was hungry for her, hungry to bolster the connection between them. When she took him inside her with such sweetness in the carriage, all his boredom and restlessness had vanished. She thrilled him as no woman ever had. Tupping Selina Martin was fiercely exciting, but the greatest gift she gave him was the peace deep in his soul, a peace he'd never experienced in all his wild, wanton seekings after bliss.

"It's still early," she murmured, staring at the wineglass.

As if to confirm that statement, the mahogany clock on the mantel struck nine. They'd lingered over dinner. As if by common consent, they'd avoided contentious topics. Neither had mentioned Cecil or money, or how fast their time together would pass.

Brock enjoyed talking to Selina. He'd always appreciated women's company. He wasn't the sort of scoundrel who had no use for a mistress once he'd fucked her. Beyond his interest in Selina as his partner in sensual exploration, he liked her. He even liked her strength of character, although it had proved damned inconvenient when he offered her financial help.

As the evening progressed, it became clear that Selina considered any sacrifice worthwhile for her son's sake. She didn't view her future with Cecil in a spirit of self-pity, but with grim endurance. It was the price she paid for her child's future, and she paid it without complaint.

Brock couldn't despise her stalwart love for Gerald. Damn it, he admired it. He wished to heaven his mother had loved him with such constancy.

"Then shall we go to the drawing room?" he asked with a distinct lack of enthusiasm.

He wanted her in his arms. He didn't want to wait. But on the other hand, he didn't want her to think he was a man without any graces at all.

Her faint smile only deepened her air of mystery. He bit back a groan. His interest in swiving her heightened by the second.

She lifted her gaze and stared straight at him. The heat in her eyes shot a bolt of lust right to his balls. "I'd rather go upstairs and...fuck."

The sound of the profanity in her soft, precise voice made him see stars. "Selina..." he choked out, as his hands fisted on the damask tablecloth.

She watched him, her eyes devouring him, as if he was even more delicious than Mary's *bœuf en daube*. "I want you." The wry humor, that proved such a beguiling surprise now he came to know her, gleamed in her eyes. "I want you in a bed where I don't feel like I'm going to end up on the floor if the carriage hits a bump."

He gave an appreciative grunt of laughter. "That was all part of the experience."

Her bold, assessing gaze focused on him again and made his balls tighten. At this rate, she'd be lucky if she escaped a fast tumble on the dining table. "I'm sure you'll think of something else to keep me occupied."

His laugh this time held a touch of surprise. "No doubt I will. I am a notorious rake after all." He paused. "I like that you're not shy."

Color edged her cheekbones, putting the lie to that statement. "We don't have time for coyness."

"Aye, that's true." A slow smile curled his lips. Selina had surprised him from the first, and she kept surprising him. No wonder he found her so damned enchanting. He stood and held out his hand. "Shall we?"

She surveyed him as if he was the best thing she'd ever seen in her life. He knew she had no idea how her expression betrayed her, but every time her eyes lit with pleasure at the sight of him, she knocked another chip off the cynicism encasing his heart. He'd had so many lovers, but he already knew this was the lover he'd miss all his life.

Taking his hand, she rose with the natural grace that had drawn his attention the first time he saw her. "We shall."

He drew her into his arms for a kiss. At the first touch of her lips, the air caught fire. She'd left last night's innocent hesitation far behind. This was a woman who knew what she wanted. The searing candor of her desire sizzled through him like lightning.

By the time they drew apart, he was shaking. So was she. She had that lovely dazzled astonishment on her face that always made him want to kiss her again. Which, by God, he couldn't do. If he kissed her here, Mary would never get in to clean up. And upstairs, as Selina had been brazen enough to point out, there was a large bed. A bed he'd never shared with a lover. It seemed appropriate that the one woman who would sleep with him there was the one woman he'd never forget.

On a practical level, as she also noted, a bed offered privacy and potential that his carriage lacked, however incendiary their exploits on the way to the hunting box.

"I want to run," she said with a breathless laugh.

"Do you want me to chase you, you wee hussy?"

"You know…" She paused as though she contemplated the secrets of the ages, before a joyous giggle escaped her. She whipped out of his arms and darted for the door. "I think I do!"

Between her head start and his surprise at discovering this playful aspect to her character, he didn't catch up until he reached the landing off the bedrooms. "Devil take you, you're quick," he said breathlessly, as he hauled her into his arms for another passionate kiss.

He loved the sound of her laughter, carefree and bright. "No, you're slow. You're not used to doing the chasing."

By God, she might be right. Too many easy victories left him spoiled. No wonder that until he met Selina, he was bored and utterly sick of himself.

"Now I've caught you, what the devil am I going to do with you?"

"Take me to bed, Brock," she whispered. As the laughter faded from her eyes, he read a craving as potent as his own. "I need you. I need you now."

"My darling…" he said, moved by her honesty.

Words escaped him as he swung her up into his arms and covered the distance to the bedroom in a few swift paces. He shouldered open the door and set Selina down in the center of the room.

Outside, the snow had set in, but here in this room, fire blazed in the hearth and blue velvet curtains enclosed them in cozy warmth. He stepped back. "Let me see you. You've no idea how often I've imagined you naked."

She cast him a knowing glance. "I can guess."

"The moment I saw you, so subdued and beautiful, you took over my every thought. You still do."

Pleasure softened her features, made her so lovely he couldn't believe his good fortune in winning her. "And I saw you, so striking and tall and handsome – and wicked. I hated that I wasn't the sort of woman who would ever attract your notice. Even though attracting your notice put my whole future at risk."

He felt a satisfied smile curve his lips. "Now you're a rake's mistress."

"And I've never been happier."

Unaccustomed emotion cracked his heart. She was such a superb woman. She ought to have the world at her feet. Yet her expectations for happiness were so humble.

Now wasn't the moment to dwell on whether she deserved better than this week of self-indulgence. Passion beckoned too powerfully. He waved at that becoming arrangement of upswept curls.

"Take down your hair. I've dreamed of seeing your hair flowing about you." Detailed, sensual dreams where tresses of rich blonde draped across his bare skin like ropes of silk.

The softness lingered in her eyes, as she sidled closer to the dressing table. The mirror behind her offered him two views of her, tall and slim and lovely.

With more of that grace that stole his breath, she raised her arms and began to slide the pins from her hair.

They'd rushed up here like children promised cake. Now Brock felt like they had all the time in the world. Selina must feel the same, because her movements were unhurried as she removed each pin and placed it on the dressing table.

A long lock unraveled over her shoulder, then another. The tresses uncoiled one by one, until a veil of hair covered her shoulders. His blood began to beat a pounding tattoo of need. He stepped back to lean against the bed, fumbling behind him to curl his fingers over the elaborately carved baseboard.

His hunger was devilish sweet. He'd wanted enough women in his life to know that this keen craving was a gift.

"Run your hands through it," he said in a harsh voice, as his gaze ate up the cascade of hair. It was long and thick, cloaking her to the waist. In the mirror, it rippled down her back, hinting at russet and gold and flaxen blonde.

Building need turned her eyes dark. The urge rose to grab her and rip off her clothes and slake himself in her. But stronger yet was the urge to linger on each moment. Later they'd have the chance for a fast coupling.

This first time she uncovered her body for him, he didn't want his greedy impulses to rule. He wanted to treasure each moment like a pearl threaded onto a necklace. So when she left him, he kept this exquisite memory of every step in her surrender to take out and cherish.

As if under a spell, she obeyed. The flush on her skin and the erratic susurration of her breath told him that undoing her hair in front of him excited her, too. She lifted the heavy weight of hair and released it to drift about her.

Brock heaved a lengthy sigh born in appreciation and rising arousal. His hands clutched the baseboard as he battled not to step forward and snatch up handfuls of that silky glory.

"I want to see you naked," he said in a choked voice.

She surveyed him with eyes luminous with desire. "I've never been naked for a man before." Her voice was low and husky and made his skin tighten for want of her.

"Are you afraid?"

When she shook her head, that mass of hair shifted around her. "No."

"No?"

"Perhaps a little." A faint smile lengthened her lips. "But I'm glad that my first time is with you."

Painful emotion stabbed him. Only Selina had this power to slice through his physical yearning. She was so vulnerable. Yet she was powerful, too. Purity of heart made her the strongest woman he'd ever known. "Selina, you do me too much honor."

She made a bewildered gesture with one hand. "What shall I do now?"

"Let me watch you undress." His voice turned hoarse, as the prospect of seeing her unclothed shot a shuddering thrill through him.

She didn't move to cooperate, and the comprehensive glance she cast him seared like fire. "I hope you intend to return the favor."

"By God…" He straightened to reach for her, then sucked in a huge breath and told himself to wait. His roaring impatience was part of the rich mix of pleasure.

That smile flirting with her lips deepened, and he saw her uncertainty fade as she recognized the dominion she wielded over him. With taunting languor, she picked up a chair and placed it on the rich red and blue rug in the center of the room – and in the center of his view.

Selina cast him a sidelong glance, to confirm she caught his attention. As if any red-blooded man could look away. She lifted one foot to the chair and slid her skirts up to reveal the shapely legs he recalled so vividly. But there was a difference between catching a glimpse in a rattling, swaying carriage and now, when time spun away from them along a bright path.

His gaze traced the neat ankle in its white stocking and the taut calf. Up to the sweet little knee and the pretty blue garter he'd already remarked upon. Pale, slender thighs disappeared into a tumble of skirts. A growl of hunger escaped him, and he tightened his grip on the baseboard.

He expected her to fumble with the ribbon around her ankles as she removed her shoe. But while his turmoil grew, she seemed to become calmer. Blood thrummed like thunder in his ears as she took off the blue satin slipper, then untied her garter to slide the fragile stocking down.

Even her feet were pretty. His eyes feasted on the high arch and the small toes. By the time she did the same with the other leg, he was in such a lather, he was close to forgetting his own name.

Brock retained just enough sense to notice at least one thing. "You're not wearing drawers," he forced out of a tight throat.

She lowered her foot from the chair and faced him. To his regret, her skirts slid down to lend her a spurious modesty. "No."

"I wish I'd known when we had dinner."

This smile was sly with sensual awareness. "I thought you might like a surprise."

"I do." His voice scraped out. Only she had the power to steal his ability to speak. "Don't."

She raised her eyebrows. "Don't?"

"While we're together, don't wear them."

When her eyes met his, he saw that this teasing game lured her to the brink of madness, too. "Very well."

Satisfaction filled him. He gestured toward her gown. "The dress next."

"You'll have to help me. It does up the back."

"You want me to play your maid?"

"Yes."

Brock straightened. His cock swelled against his breeches. She already knew that. When she'd completed that slow inspection, her attention had lingered on his arousal. "Come here then. Although I can't promise I'll be too deft."

"Shall I call Mary?"

"No, damn you."

Selina gave a brief laugh and sauntered across with a sway of her hips that heated his blood. "Here, my lord."

She turned and bundled that wealth of hair up in both hands so he could reach her lacing. He leaned in and breathed deep of her jasmine scent, before he worked at the back of the dress. With each inch of flesh he uncovered across her shoulders, need escalated.

He forced himself to concentrate. The task took far too long, but at last the gown gaped open to reveal stays over a sheer white shift.

Brock told himself he wouldn't touch her while she undressed, but he couldn't resist placing his mouth on the graceful curve where her neck met her shoulder. She released a long sigh of surrender as he scraped his teeth over the sensitive flesh.

For a luscious moment, she sagged against him. Then she straightened and stepped away.

"What about your corset?" he asked, voice raw with desire.

When she bent her head, he stifled the urge to taste the nape of her neck. "It hooks in the front. I can do it."

Probably better she did. This drawn-out seduction became unmitigated torture. "I want to see your breasts."

Without turning around, she wriggled out of the gown and let it pool at her bare feet. His eyes feasted on the rear view of Selina wearing only her undergarments and that extravagant wealth of hair.

All the moisture dried from his mouth when she untied the tapes holding her petticoats and they slipped down to froth at her feet. The white globes of her buttocks pressed against the frail shift. His hands curled into fists, as another jolt of arousal shook him. His breath emerged in rough gasps.

She stepped away just before the temptation to shape that round softness overcame him. When she turned, the view from the front was even more enticing than the view from the back. The corset pushed up her breasts. Dark pink nipples, hard and needy, were visible under the linen. The loose shift hinted at shadowy secrets between her legs.

The long delay must eat at her, too, because her hands were clumsy with haste as she ripped at the hooks down the front of her plain corset. If she was his and not just a temporary lover, he'd array her in underclothing to make a courtesan blush. That magnificent figure deserved a magnificent setting.

His anticipation rose as she slid the corset off and dropped it on the floor beside the rest of her clothes. Then with a determined air, she grabbed her shift and hauled it over her head. As she tossed this last garment aside, she raised her chin.

"You beggar my dreams," he whispered in awe. He straightened, his gaze fixed on her. "You're perfect."

"I want to be perfect for you, Brock." Her features were stark with need. "I want to cut so deep into your soul that you never forget me as long as you live."

"You have," he muttered, too overcome to hide the truth.

His gaze traveled over her creamy curves, the high breasts with their crests beaded with arousal. The plain of her stomach above the nest of golden brown curls.

Color tinged her cheeks, but she remained unmoving as he stepped closer. He brushed the fall of hair back from her shoulders, until he gained an unhindered view of her body.

His touch was light, even as devils of lust and possessiveness warred inside him. He skimmed his hands down her arms and along her spine and felt the quiver that belied her defiant stance.

Deliberately, he didn't touch her breasts. He caught up one silky skein of hair and brought it to his lips. Her scent rose to his nostrils, rich and heady, tinged with jasmine. With a hum of pleasure, he rubbed the silky tress against his face. She made a choked sound and leaned forward.

His control shattered. He dragged her into his arms and kissed her with all the passion he'd leashed until this moment. She twined her arms around him and pressed closer with an untamed hunger that made his blood pump hot and hard.

He swung her in his arms until she bumped into the bed and collapsed back in a beguiling jumble of bare arms and legs and drifting hair. He didn't follow her down. Instead, he ripped off his neck cloth and coat and flung them aside.

She watched him, eyes avid with hunger. "More," she said in a low growl that threatened to set him alight.

His laugh betrayed a crack. "I'm madam's obedient servant."

"Good." She lifted herself on her elbows so she could see him better. The movement jostled those lush breasts.

Before she came to him, he'd wondered whether she'd be a timid lover, reluctant to step outside the bounds of propriety. He loved how wrong he'd been.

Now Selina made no attempt to cover her nakedness but seemed to bask in his admiration. He took a moment to relish the sight of her white body sprawled over the sheets. Her wild mane of hair fanned about her in rippling amber and flax.

Brock shed his waistcoat and shirt in a hurry. When he stood before her bare-chested, she released a voluptuous sigh of appreciation. "You're a beautiful man, Lord Bruard."

For years, women had told him he was handsome, but the sheer wonder in Selina's tone had him blushing. That hadn't happened since he was a boy in the Highlands, chasing his first lassies. "Thank you," he said gruffly.

She raised her hand in a languid gesture. "My pleasure."

He chuckled. "That sounds like an invitation."

That luscious mouth with its full lower lip curled in a wicked smile that a day ago he'd never have imagined he'd see on prim Mrs. Selina Martin's face.

"Clever as well as decorative. What a lucky girl I am." She must have seen he was on the verge of jumping on her – hell, he was so ready for her, he was close to coming. Only the memory of this afternoon's wretched overexcitement and its result held him back. "But not yet."

"You're torturing me," he groaned.

The smug little cat laughed. "You'll live." When her attention sharpened below his waist, the results were predictable. "More."

Brock dropped into the chair she'd used to such devastating effect when she'd removed her shoes and stockings. He couldn't imagine he looked half so appealing as he tugged off his boots and stood to shed his breeches.

She shifted to rest upon the pillows piled high against the headboard. Her gaze fastened on his rampant cock. He'd thought he was already as hard as he could get, but unbelievably he experienced a fresh rush of arousal.

The silence extended.

"Selina?"

When she licked her lips, he groaned again. Still she didn't speak.

After a bristling interval, he asked, "Have I shocked you into a trance?"

To his relief, her intense expression eased. "Did I say you're beautiful? I was wrong."

"You were?"

"Oh, yes." He was sure now that whatever her reaction to his nakedness, disappointment wasn't the problem. "I think splendid is a much better word."

"Selina..."

She smiled and held out a hand remarkable for its steadiness. "Now come here and do splendid things to me before I die of wanting you."

CHAPTER SEVEN

Selina watched vivid excitement flood Brock's dark features. She didn't exaggerate when she called him splendid. All that masculine strength. All that masculine potency. How could she resist?

"My darling girl..." In two strides, he reached the bed and came down over her. She framed his narrow hips between her legs and curled her arms around his supple back. His muscles tautened beneath her touch.

She starved for him to thrust into her. He was starving, too. She could smell his need on his skin.

"You're as hot as a fire," she said in wonder, stroking down his spine to clasp his firm male buttocks with eager hands.

"You make me burn."

She believed it. His eyes glittered with desire, and his rod was an insistent presence against her soft belly.

He kissed her hard, if too briefly, but she forgave him when he began to nip and nuzzle at her neck. Roderick had never kissed her there. Roderick had been interested in accomplishing the deed without undue effort. She'd had no idea that such a universe of pleasure awaited in another man's arms. With every scrape of Brock's teeth, every brush of Brock's lips, thrills sizzled through her and the pulsing, needy weight between her legs grew more urgent.

She arched up with a broken moan, a silent plea for more. When he'd pushed inside her in the carriage, she felt complete for the first time in her life. She couldn't wait to experience that glory again. The shift in position brushed the aching tips of her breasts across the light covering of dark hair on his chest, and the tickling friction set her aquiver with arousal.

"Brock, please..." she said, unable to put into words what she wanted.

He raised his head from where he tormented her to madness and stared down into her face. His green eyes were as dark as a forest pond. "I've never wanted a woman the way I want you, Selina."

A warm rush of pleasure washed over her, heightening her desire. "I want you now," she rasped out.

His lips curled with the hint of teasing that always made her melt. She'd never imagined that the act of love could encompass light as well as darkness. Brock had promised her joy. With him, she discovered joy had many faces, beyond the cataclysm of sexual climax.

"Soon."

Despite her urgency, she smiled back. "You're a tormenting beggar."

"I want to taste your breasts first. They've fueled my dreams, too."

His honesty drew a confession from her. "I've often imagined your hands on me."

His soft, surprised laugh bumped her deeper into the mattress beneath her back. "Have you indeed, you naughty lass?"

"I...I imagined you doing a lot of things to me."

"My darling..." He bent his head and traced a path of fire across her shoulder and down the slope of her breast. Her nipples tightened to the point of pain, and she bowed up in wordless encouragement.

He shifted and caught her breasts in his hands, drawing a hiss of pleasure from her as he squeezed. Then overpowering sensation vanquished her ability to breathe, as he drew one yearning nipple between his lips and brushed his thumb across the other.

Roderick had been rough, tugging on her nipples with painful enthusiasm. Brock's touch was much more subtle. Gentle suckling on the tip made her sigh, and his hands were careful. Soon gentleness faded, and the wash of delight transformed into restless longing that had her gasping and writhing. She buried her hands in the rumpled silk of his hair and stretched up for more of that fiendish delight. His tongue laved her nipple, then she started as his teeth scraped over the sensitive flesh. A ribbon of flame licked down from her breast to her constricting womb.

By the time he raised his head, she was quaking as if she had a fever. Her vision was misty with almost unbearable arousal.

"You have beautiful breasts, Selina. My dreams didn't do you justice."

"My dreams didn't do you justice either," she admitted, running her hand down the side of his face. He'd shaved before dinner, but now soft whiskers prickled her palm. "Please, I need you inside me. Don't wait any longer. I ache for you."

His smile this time was tender. "Let me ease your need."

"You do," she said on an exhalation, angling her hips in unabashed demand. "I crave you."

He lifted himself on his elbows until he could see her face. His gaze unwavering, he pushed forward with a smoothness that still astonished her. This was their first day as lovers, yet there was no awkwardness, no jostling to find their connection. Instead, there was this transcendent closeness, as though every time Brock joined with her, he claimed her soul.

Her overstimulated body clenched into immediate climax, closing hard around him. As she rode out the turbulent waves, she cried out again and dug her fingernails into his shoulders.

Brock groaned and buried his head in the curve of her neck, grazing her with his teeth. She was shuddering with reaction when Brock began to move, the powerful possession stoking her wild rapture.

Selina was breathless and trembling as she drifted down from the heights. Then to her amazement, response flickered to life once more, as Brock set up a deep, driving rhythm that crushed her into the bed. After such a climax, she would have thought rising to another so swiftly was impossible, but soon she was shaking. He kept moving within her, penetrating so deep that she felt he took ownership of every inch of her.

The next time, her womb contracted before she even recovered from the previous ascent. She rose to meet him, kissing him with all the passion she felt.

At last, his superhuman control showed signs of shredding. He groaned again and caught her hips, tilting her. The new angle fired off a fresh volley of fireworks. She moaned and clutched tight to Brock's shoulders, slick with sweat.

As his movements grew choppy, she toppled over to take another flight among the stars. Through the raging oceans in her ears, she was vaguely aware of a deep, guttural sound coming from his throat.

He ripped himself away, shaking and sweating, and his body jerked over and over as he pumped his seed onto her bare stomach. She shivered with wanton excitement, as hot semen splattered across her skin.

Brock rolled to the side and collapsed beside her with a lengthy, broken groan that conveyed both weariness and completion. She slumped back against the rumpled sheets, boneless with exhaustion.

Selina supposed that she should get up and wash. But she was as limp as a piece of wet string. She felt as if she'd flown into the center of the sun and dissolved into blinding light.

"I had no idea you could do that to me," she said in a croaky voice, once she'd recovered breath enough to speak. "I had no idea anyone could do that to me."

He flung one arm over his eyes, and his chest heaved as he struggled to fill his lungs. Had what they'd just done tested his limits, too? Surely not. "But you knew about pleasure."

The ecstatic daze receded, and she stiffened with wariness. "I…"

He lowered his arm and turned his head until he could see her. "You said Roderick had no idea how to give you a climax."

A grim smile turned down her lips. "He might have had some idea. But if he did, he never exerted himself to prove it." She paused as she thought back to those uncomfortable, disheartening encounters with her husband. "I wonder if he did know. The women he paid for sexual congress wouldn't demand any particular consideration, I suspect."

"Yet he's been the only man in your bed."

Selina frowned up at the stars and moons embroidered on the tester above the bed. "I told you he was." All of a sudden, she felt awkward. "Don't you believe me?"

He rolled onto his side and rose on one elbow. "If you succumbed to temptation, I'm in no position to point a finger. In fact, I'd rather admire you if you did. That oaf Roderick deserved some of his own medicine."

When Brock was buried between her thighs and she moaned and twisted in the throes of pleasure, she hadn't felt self-conscious. Right now, she was ready to die of embarrassment. Her cheeks were hot, and she was agonizingly aware of her nakedness and the sticky mess drying on her stomach.

With a shaking hand, she grabbed for the sheet. "I told you that I never betrayed my vows. That was the truth. I had a son to consider. A notorious mother could do him harm."

Brock reached to catch her wrist, stopping her from hauling the sheet up to hide her mortification. "I'm not judging you, Selina."

She avoided his eyes and tried to pull free. "It sounds like you are."

"I'm curious. Damn it, I want to know everything about you. It's absurd, but I want to encompass a whole lifetime with you in the space of one short week. You don't have to tell me anything you don't want to. You owe me nothing. We come together by free will, and I have no right to compel you. But I'm puzzled. I hadn't expected you to understand what a climax is."

"I've never known pleasure at a man's hand until you," she mumbled. She wasn't comfortable with his questions, although the bewildered desperation in his tone mollified her a little. This ferocious need that flowered between them left her reeling. She was gratified to know that the worldly roué also found himself at a loss.

"I believe you." When he drew her hand to his lips to place a kiss on the knuckles, she didn't resist. "Let me clean you up."

"I can look after myself." Her voice retained that tart edge.

"Let me," he said softly, and the glow in his eyes vanquished her brief umbrage. "I want to cherish you."

Cherish... What a lovely word. One she couldn't apply to the way either Roderick or Cecil treated her. "Very well."

Brock's kiss was gentle. He swung out of bed, utterly at ease with his nudity. With deep feminine pleasure, she watched him walk to the washstand, admiring the long horseman's thighs and the way the tight buttocks flexed as he strode across the carpet. The flickering candlelight turned his smooth olive skin to gold.

"I scratched you," she said in horror, as her attention fastened on the jagged red marks marring that supple back.

Without turning, he lifted the jug and splashed some water into the bowl. "I know."

"I'm sorry."

"I'm not. I like to wear your mark."

Pleasure made her curl her toes against the sheets. How could she defend herself against him when he kept saying these things that set her heart cartwheeling?

Defying the way her tired muscles objected, she pushed herself higher against the pillows and watched as he washed with quick efficiency. There was something thrilling about sharing such an intimate moment with him.

Watching him wash his member brought back memories of having him deep inside her. A shiver of profound pleasure rippled through her. Already she wanted him again. He turned her into a glutton for his body.

After he'd dried himself, he emptied the bowl, then filled it again and carried it across to the bed. "At least I can do a better job this time than I managed in the carriage."

"You don't have to act my servant."

The tenderness tinging his smile made her want to cry. Which was mad, after the most joyous experience of her life. But she knew Brock well enough to recognize that while passion was nothing new to him, perhaps this poignant sweetness was.

"Let me care for you."

She stretched out against the crumpled sheets. "I'm not used to people seeking my comfort."

His features darkened, and those expressive black brows lowered over his arrogant blade of a nose. Another surge of emotion overwhelmed her. She wasn't used to people being angry on her behalf either.

"While you're with me, you're my priority."

He dipped the flannel into the bowl and began to wipe her stomach. While the water was only lukewarm, it felt glorious on her skin. Or perhaps it felt glorious because Brock did the honors.

"I hate that life is such a lonely fight for you, Selina," he murmured, concentrating on washing her. "I'd change that if I could."

Brock cut straight to her core, so deep and with such ease. She blinked back foolish tears. She had no idea he'd guessed so much about her life without him.

Oh, dear. With every moment, the bond between them strengthened, defied her claim that this affair was a matter of physical attraction alone. She was in such trouble here. And she had no idea how to fix it.

At Derwent Hall, she'd spoken so blithely about choosing a lover who wouldn't fall in love with her. But what if she fell in love herself? Selina didn't want to leave Essex with a broken heart. After a mere day in Brock's company, she feared it might already be too late to save herself.

As if he hadn't changed her world in a few simple words, he rinsed the flannel and began to run it over her breasts. His tender care thrilled her to her soul.

"Things...things aren't so bad as that," she stammered.

Amusement kicked up one corner of the thin mouth that she'd once thought rather cruel. She didn't think that now. "Liar."

She didn't argue, because what could she say when dreary duty was all that life had offered her? Except for Gerald. "I find happiness in my son. It's something."

Brock's lips flattened. He lifted one arm and washed that, too, paying attention to her hands and fingers. Nobody had washed her since she was a child. This didn't feel at all like that. "Not enough."

"It has to be." A world of regret burdened her words. "Now at least I'll have the memories of a week in a rake's arms."

He lifted her other arm and ran the damp flannel from shoulder to wrist. "I wish..."

No, Selina couldn't bear to hear him say it. If she let herself wish for more, it would crush her. She couldn't even let him say the words. More tears stung her eyes, but she blinked them back. After

Wednesday, she'd have plenty of time to cry. A lifetime.

She reached over and caught his hand. "Don't."

"I'm sorry." He shook his head. "It's just…"

"I know," she said in a choked voice and closed eyes that ached with the weight of moisture dammed behind the lids.

She heard him rinse the cloth again, the splash of the water a soft counterpoint to her uneven breathing. She felt the damp cloth on her thighs, before Brock parted her legs and began to wash her sex.

"You leave me no modesty," she muttered.

Selina opened her eyes to see him smiling again. It seemed a less convincing effort than usual, but she appreciated that he drew back from talking about the end of their affair. Already she was too aware of how short their time together was. More reason not to poison their few days with fretting about the ending that sped toward them.

"Modesty is overrated."

He wasn't touching her with any hint of lechery, yet her oversensitive flesh sent messages of sexual pleasure leaping through her. By the time he finished, she was trembling.

After he dropped the flannel into the bowl, he bent to kiss her just above the damp curls covering her mound. More tenderness. The stomach beneath this tribute clenched in an agony of longing.

Brock shifted away to set the bowl on the washstand and returned holding a linen towel. As he dried her with an attention and thoroughness that roused more of that painful need, she sought some distraction from her wicked longings.

She asked him something that she'd wondered about since she first saw him. "What were you like as a boy?"

Another of those intriguing half-smiles. Heaven help her, he was a handsome man. Selina was always aware of his surpassing physical attractions, but sometimes, like now, his beauty pierced her sharp as an arrow. The softness in the face she'd once thought hard and ruthless made him look younger, more approachable. The tumble of dark hair, the glow in his eyes, and the powerful, long-limbed body stole her breath.

He returned to hang the towel on its rail. "I was a little horror."

She could imagine he'd been spoiled. He was a beautiful man. He would have been a gorgeous child. What mother could resist smothering him with love and attention and gifts?

"Full of mischief, no doubt."

"I had my moments." In an action of breathtaking smoothness, he hooked up his breeches from the floor and slid them on. It reminded her of her nakedness. Odd how comfortable she felt unclothed in his company. It seemed natural to allow him every liberty.

When Selina slipped out of bed, she couldn't restrain a groan. No man had touched her in years, and today's exuberant sexual activity set long-disused muscles protesting at the sudden movement.

Brock paused in the act of pouring two glasses of wine from the decanter on the cabinet near the door. "Are you all right?"

As she recalled the day that she'd just spent, heat tinged her cheeks. "I'm not used to such...vigorous exercise."

He gave an appreciative grunt and went back to filling the glasses. "I'll get you into shape."

Into shape? Selina had a feeling she'd leave here as a completely new person.

She bent to collect her crumpled shift from the floor and tug it over her head. "I need to get back on the horse?"

Humor lit his expression as he turned to face her, carrying the two glasses. "Back on something, at any rate."

She gave a low chuckle as she accepted the wine and sank down onto a leather chair in front of the roaring fire. The room was so deliciously warm, it was hard to imagine it was snowing outside like the end of the world.

"So where did you grow up?" she asked, unwilling to let him wriggle away from her question. He'd admitted to a hunger to know all about her. At the very least, her interest in him rivaled his in her.

Brock wandered over to the window and pulled back the blue curtains to reveal a Stygian blackness. He sipped his wine and stared out with a pensive expression. "At Bruard. It's quite as spectacular as it sounds. A man can breathe there."

"You love it."

An enigmatic smile hovered about his lips. "I do."

"When were you last there?"

He closed the heavy velvet curtains and turned from the window. "Five years ago."

Shocked, puzzled, she studied Brock. More was going on here than she understood. "That seems...a long time."

He shrugged and took another mouthful of wine.

Selina could take a hint, even if with some reluctance. He had a right to his secrets. As did she.

She sampled her wine, a fine claret, and stared into the fire. What a day this had been. Unlike any day she'd passed before. Sexual satisfaction was a lazy beat in her blood and for once, the constant fear that had been her companion for so many years receded. Life with all its problems lurked in wait, but something in this quiet, luxurious room made her feel safe. At least for the moment.

"For a woman who drives me out of my mind with lust, you can be a damned restful presence," Brock murmured from where he remained near the window.

Startled, she looked up. She was tired, pleasantly so, and she'd drifted off into a reverie crammed with memories of all the depraved things she and Brock had done. "You don't sound very pleased about that."

"I'm not." He sighed and crossed the room to put his half-full glass on the mantelpiece. "It makes a man devilish prone to confidences."

If he hadn't sounded so tolerant and so affectionate, she might have taken offense. She'd drunk even less of her wine than he had of his. She set it on the small table at her elbow. "I have no right to pry."

He ran his hand through his mass of black hair and released an impatient exhalation. "If you did, I'd tell you to go to Hades."

Another silence fell. When he began to speak, his voice was low and uncharacteristically hesitant. She did her best to hide her curiosity. In her experience, he wasn't a man who was ever hesitant. "My father died about ten years ago. My mother died when I was fifteen."

"I'm sorry, Brock." Selina wanted to rise and take him in her arms, but something in his bristling tension kept her sitting just where she was.

"So am I." He paused, his features hardening. He went back to looking like the cynical, heartless rake she'd first thought him. "Not that she was ever much of a mother."

Selina didn't speak, just watched him steadily.

Again, her silence lured him into explaining further. "She was very beautiful. And wild. And selfish. And destructive to anyone who fell under her spell. God knows, if I was to count the victims of her flightiness, the poor beggars would line the road from here to the Highlands. I take after her."

Selina had already realized that Brock was a complex man with a complex past that she couldn't pretend to understand. Even so, she was surprised and distressed to hear such self-hatred tainting his voice.

She frowned, considering what he'd said. "Only the beauty." She paused. "And the wildness." She didn't fool herself that this was a domesticated animal she'd caught for herself, however fleetingly.

He shot her a half-smiling glance that cut to the quick. "I'm no hero."

She shrugged. "Perhaps not, but you're a better man than I think you recognize."

A dismissive grunt greeted that statement. "I doubt it."

She shook her head with a stubborn certainty that emerged from the depths of her being. "I don't. You might have done a thousand wicked things in your life. In fact, I'll warrant you have. But at heart, you're not a wicked man. You're kind – at least you've been kind to me. Nor are you only wrapped up in yourself. You also have some honor. It would be easy to ignore my request not to give me a child. I'm sure it would be more enjoyable for you if you did, and I've been in no position to stop you. Yet you stuck to your promise." She made a helpless gesture. "We've only been together a day, yet I could give you a hundred examples of your consideration."

He looked taken aback, which made her want to laugh. It seemed praise for his character rather than his physical appearance left him nonplussed. "I'm counted a profligate and a seducer and woefully unreliable. I've left a trail of broken hearts all over England."

"I'm sure that's true." She had a horrid premonition that she'd add her heart to that list, once she left him. "But it's not the whole truth."

Self-deprecating humor twisted his lips. "If I was as principled as you say, I'd now try to talk you out of that unjustified assessment of my character."

"Don't bother. You won't succeed."

He shook his head with more of that fond disbelief that made her ache with yearning. She fast became besotted with Brock Drummond, heaven save her. "You're an obstinate wee thing. I wonder if Cecil knows."

"I doubt it," she said shortly.

"He doesn't know you at all, does he?"

The reminder of what awaited once she left this den of sin wasn't welcome. Dejected, she went back to staring into the fire. "He doesn't care to. That doesn't mean I won't be a good wife to him."

"For Gerald's sake."

"Yes."

"Because you love your son."

Something in Brock's tone drew her attention. "You know, for a heartless rake, you talk about love a lot."

She expected him to react to the accusation with horror, but again he surprised her. "I do, don't I?"

Another silence wrapped around them. Something in this room encouraged intimate revelations. Perhaps because it was warm and enclosed, and outside the world was cold and dangerous and unforgiving.

Brock turned away and kneeled to poke at the fire until it was roaring. When he rose, he leaned an arm on the mantel and watched the flames with a moody expression. God help her, even masculine sulks looked spectacular on him.

When at last he spoke, he didn't look up. "My mother didn't love me."

Appalled, Selina stared at him. Everything in her rejected his flat statement. "I don't believe that."

The gaze Brock settled on her was bleak. "Nevertheless it's true."

"Then she was a fool," Selina said sharply.

Because while this complicated man might have his faults, however good he'd been to her, he was eminently lovable. Too much so for her peace of mind.

"Gerald is lucky."

She frowned, not following the connection. "I wouldn't say so. His father gave no thought to his future, and it's never lucky to lose a parent so young, however feckless that parent might be."

"But he has you." Brock turned his attention back to the fire, she suspected for his pride's sake. He must know how much this conversation revealed.

"Well, of course."

"Once you pledge your loyalty, you never falter."

Pity flooded her. Because it sounded like his mother had never put her child ahead of her entertainment. "I try to stand by my word."

"And you'd do anything for your son."

"Yes." Although guilt added a rancid taste to the avowal. This affair threatened Gerald's future, and she couldn't pretend that she was here for anything other than selfish gratification.

Selina studied the man who had lured her into sin and for once, her hunger for the pleasure he gave her wasn't paramount. Instead she felt a need to comfort him that was so overwhelming, it was agonizing. Because right now, the man who brooded into the fire wasn't the emperor of all he surveyed. He wasn't heartless and invincible and beyond the reach of human frailty. Brock turned out to be vulnerable in a way she'd never imagined possible at the Derwents' house, when she'd observed the handsome rake, the cynosure of all eyes. Eyes brazenly covetous or envious or disapproving. Eyes that she realized saw nothing of the real man.

"I'm so sorry that you didn't know a mother's love. That's a wound nothing can heal." She held out her hand. "Now stop looming over me and come here."

After giving her one of those sweet smiles that always threatened to break her heart, he crossed to fold himself down on the floor at her feet. "I never talk about this."

He leaned against her knee, warm and solid and somehow more real after sharing those reluctant revelations. She ran her fingers through his untidy black hair in an attempt to soothe his unhappiness. "Thank you for telling me."

"I don't know why the hell I did. My maudlin tale hardly promotes me in your mind as your irresistible demon lover."

Keeping up the gentle stroking, she smiled. She recalled likening him to a big, predatory cat. Right now, she wanted to make him purr, although it was just as possible that he'd hiss and claw, especially if he discovered the deep well of compassion he'd opened inside her. He wouldn't appreciate her pity. She had her own pride. She understood his.

"You can go back to being my demon lover tomorrow," she murmured and was pleased to hear him respond with a huff of grudging amusement. "So Bruard holds too many unhappy memories for you."

He sighed and rested against her a little more heavily. "Aye. Which is mad because Mamma spent as little time there as she could, until she was too ill to manage in London any longer."

When she'd crawled back to the one place that wouldn't deny her shelter, Selina thought with a flash of spite. She assumed the late Countess of Bruard had been unhappy – that was the most sympathetic view she could take of someone who neglected her child so shamefully. Unless she'd just been cold and self-centered and careless about the damage she left behind. Whatever the reasons for her behavior, Selina couldn't forgive the woman.

"How did your father react?"

Another grunt of amusement. Grimmer this time. "Not well, as you'd expect. But he was a bloodless, upright, self-righteous sod. If he hadn't tried to keep my mother on such a short leash, I wonder if she'd have gone quite so far to the bad. On the other hand, she bedded any fellow who took her fancy and flaunted her infidelities in Papa's face. No man can countenance that."

Selina's hand stopped stroking him, as she struggled to comprehend the horrors of Brock's childhood. "And you were caught in the middle. How horrid. I'm surprised your father didn't do his best to turn you into a copy of himself. He must have wanted to counter your mother's pernicious influence over you."

"Aye, he did. But I'm enough like her to rebel at the whip and the spur."

She already knew that. Brock was a man who would respond to the lure of a reward, but bullying would only drive him to greater excesses. She came to understand how the wicked Lord Bruard, who had so much good in him, had become a byword for vice.

He went on in a hard voice. "Literally the whip. When every other effort failed, he tried to beat virtue into me."

"Oh, Brock," she said, trailing her hand down and gripping his shoulder. She tried to share her strength, when it was too late by twenty years to save that confused, wretched child. "I think I hate your parents."

"I think I do, too. I certainly hated my father. My mother was wayward, but at least she was alive. Papa was nothing but a dry, preachy stick, with no trace of generosity."

"How could you help loving her? If she was as beautiful as you are, she must have seemed like someone from a fairy story. Especially to a lonely boy growing up without a morsel of kindness or understanding."

"It wasn't all bad. The clansfolk were good to me, and I had companions on some of the surrounding estates. My cousin Fergus is the Laird of Achnasheen. Like me, he inherited young. I always enjoyed seeing him. I would have seen more of him, if my guardians hadn't sent me south to Eton when I was eleven."

"That must be why you don't sound very Scottish."

"Aye. And of course, once I was old enough to chase the lassies..."

She couldn't stifle a sigh, although this part of his story wasn't news to her. "They were good to you, too. And women have continued to be good to you."

Had any of it made up for those early years with two unfeeling idiots who had done him such harm? She doubted it.

He lifted his head to stare into her face. "Do you mind?"

Astonished, she met searching green eyes. "It's not my place to mind."

Something in the gaze he turned up in her direction said that her answer disappointed him. But she did her best not to think of her negligible place in the long list of Lord Bruard's conquests.

"Forget whether it's your place, do you mind?"

She frowned down at him. "Do you want me to be jealous of your other lovers?"

"Jealousy is a frightful bore."

"Exactly."

"So it seems mad to want you to be jealous."

Her hand clenched on his shoulder. "I don't understand."

"I don't either." He'd looked down so she couldn't see his face, but he sounded discontented. "Yet I find myself feeling dashed possessive when I think of you. I loathe that you're leaving me to go to another man's bed. I was hoping that perhaps you might feel a similar proprietary interest in me."

She lifted her hand away from him. His confession left her confused, troubled...elated. "Brock..."

He tilted his chin and the stare he directed at her burned through to the bone. "I know it's not fair. I know I have no rights over you, apart from the rights you grant me for the space of this week. I can't remember being jealous before. It's a damned nightmare."

She linked shaking hands in her lap. However impossible it might seem, she wasn't alone in battling to maintain some emotional detachment in this brief love affair. "We've only had a day together, and you promised passion with no deeper implications."

"Circumstances make a liar of me, then." His fierce expression didn't ease. "I find myself more involved than I've ever been with a woman."

Her spread hands indicated bewilderment, even as her imbecilic heart gloated over his taut admission. "What does that mean?"

His lips turned down with self-mockery. "For the life of me, I don't blasted well know. But I do know that if Cecil was standing before me at this minute, I'd happily drive a sword through his gizzards to stop him putting his filthy paws on you."

A guilty thrill ripped through her. At Brock's words and at the fervent light she read in his eyes. Which was mad. He declared himself a savage. She should rather chide him than revel in his turbulent desire.

"In that case, it's a good thing he's not."

"Aye. It is. Although a touch of murder might soothe my torments."

Her laugh was shocked, even as she struggled to stifle her feminine pleasure at what he said. "You must know you have no reason to envy Cecil."

Disgust flattened that expressive mouth. "Except that after Wednesday, he'll have you and I won't."

Unbelievable as it was, it seemed Brock was indeed jealous. Selina struggled to put the deplorable truth into words. "He'll never have me the way you've had me. One day with you has meant more than a lifetime with Cecil ever will. I've never felt like this before either. You've had the truest part of me, Brock. There's nobody who will ever compare with you."

Her ardent declaration didn't seem to give him any comfort. His stare remained austere. "It's not enough," he said, as he'd said earlier.

Misery clenched her throat tight. He was right. It wasn't enough.

She answered just as she had before. "It has to be."

CHAPTER EIGHT

Selina's troubled air lingered when she rose from the chair to prepare herself for sleep. She kept her shift on, Brock noticed. From where he sat on the rug near the fire, he watched her lie down in the bed where he'd recently enjoyed the most profound sexual experience of his life.

Why did this quiet woman take such a grip on his heart and senses that he longed to feast on her endlessly? Not just as his companion in pleasure. When he moved inside her, the sensation was unrivaled. But just now he'd discovered contentment in her company, knowing he found perfect understanding in her generous heart.

He wasn't a fool. From the first moment he saw her, he'd recognized that his yen for the reticent Widow Martin went beyond idle attraction. But this overmastering need astonished him, especially now he'd had her. Shallow relationships had defined his life. It was convenient to keep the bonds light between him and his lovers. So when the links snapped, as was inevitable when his attention wandered, no great damage was done.

Of course, things didn't always work as smoothly as he'd prefer, despite the conditions he always set out before an affair. Many of his paramours wanted more than a few enjoyable tumbles followed by a polite goodbye.

But until now while he might regret that he'd broken hearts, his heart had remained unscathed. After one tumultuous, ecstatic day with Selina Martin, he could already see that this time, he wouldn't walk away without a backward glance, his eyes focused on the next target.

Even more unprecedented was his need for her to see him as something beyond the eager and skillful lover. He never confided in his paramours. Tonight he'd told Selina more than he'd ever told anyone else. However painful it had been dragging up all that ancient grief, the result was more blessed peace.

Or at least he'd felt at peace until he started acting like a bloody idiot, admitting he was jealous of that undeserving bastard Cecil Canley-Smythe. Brock had suffered his lovers' jealousy too often. Not a few of the scandals attached to his name concerned discarded mistresses making trouble. Shrieking scenes, public and private, a knife attack that had left him with a scar on his arm, two attempted suicides – although neither very convincing efforts, he was grateful to say.

Not to mention the husbands who hadn't appreciated his attentions to their wives. He'd never killed a man in a duel, thank God – partly because he was always the guilty party – but he bore wounds from the field of honor. The devil must look after his own. Only that could account for Brock living long enough to make a fool of himself over Selina.

Now he felt new sympathy for his discarded mistresses and their jealous tantrums. Selina was his. The thought of her with another man burned his gut like hot acid.

If he felt like this now, God knew what state he'd be in when he took her back to the Blue Wagon. He'd be a candidate for Bedlam.

Trying to talk sense to himself and failing miserably, he wandered the room, snuffing the candles. Then he built up the fire to keep the room warm until morning. Winter in Essex could be bitter. The prospect of waking in a warm bed eased his disquiet. While the world froze outside, he'd have snuggly, sleepy Selina in his arms.

After shucking off his breeches, he slid naked into the bed. He pulled the blankets up and turned onto his side. "I'm sorry." His voice was soft. "We said we'd keep things light, and I'm spoiling that."

She remained on her back, studying him. Her gaze ate him up, as though he was a pot of hot custard and she had a tremendous appetite for pudding. Sensual interest, an incessant hum in his blood when he was with Selina, stirred to life.

"Our affair promises to be more...complicated than I imagined." A self-deprecating smile curved her soft lips. "I thought the union would be purely physical."

"I accused you of seeing me as a walking cock and nothing else."

He'd been bitter at the time. He wasn't bitter now. Perhaps because it was clear that while he swam far out into strange oceans of emotion, so did she.

"I underestimated you," she went on in a husky voice. "You're not at all the heartless rake I'd judged you to be. And I overestimated my ability to keep my feelings separate from what we do. As a temporary mistress, I'm a complete failure." Her eyes darkened with chagrin. "Yes, I am jealous of all those other women. But I don't want to be."

His restless discontentment retreated, although everything she said only made their situation more difficult. "At least I'm not alone in feeling confused."

"No, you're not alone."

He found it in himself to smile as he lay flat beside her. "Let's sleep now."

"Yes." She rose on one elbow and bent to kiss him with a searching tenderness that scraped a rift across the rusty heart that had never been at risk before. Her rich hair tumbled down around his face, firelit with gold. He tangled his hands in that opulent fall and tugged her closer.

When she drew away, emotion constricted his throat. Words jammed unspoken behind his lips, words he had no right to say, words that would shatter this idyll. Words like "stay" and "love" and "forever."

"Thank you, Brock. This has been a day I'll never forget as long as I live. I never knew such pleasure existed. I only know now because you showed me."

"Selina..." Her name forced its way past the lump blocking his throat.

As if she wanted to hear no more, she shook her head. "It's late. Let's see what tomorrow brings."

After all they'd done, she must be deuced tired. Exhaustion weighted his limbs, too. He slid his arms around her shoulders and brought her down until her head rested on his chest.

He never spent the night with a lover. Early in his career as a rake, he'd learned that sleeping beside a mistress gave her inflated ideas about where their intimacy might lead.

Selina had spent the day surprising him. Here was another surprise. He liked having her here at his side, with what remained of the night stretching ahead.

Her scent drifted over him and calmed the turmoil in his mind. The touch of her hand on his bare chest was tender, and he read trust in the way she settled beside him. He cuddled her close and despite everything, he felt that the world turned in the right direction. Selina was safe in his embrace and at this moment, she was completely his.

Brock closed his eyes, although he wasn't yet ready to sleep. The sweetness was too precious to cede it to oblivion.

She turned to lie on her side with her back to him. He pulled her closer. Through her shift, his hand cupped one full breast. Her nipple peaked against his palm, and she made a drowsy sound of encouragement.

That throaty murmur made him swell against the lush curve of her rump. He'd been half-hard since coming to bed.

For pity's sake, he was insatiable. She'd think he was a brute.

He started to pull away, but she caught his wrist and tugged his hand back to her breast. "Don't stop," she murmured in a voice heavy with weariness.

"You're tired," he said, hearing how half-hearted he sounded.

She must have heard it too, because she gave a low chuckle. "Not that tired. Fuck me, Brock."

It was his turn to give a weary laugh, as he buried his face in the warm tumble of hair. "Whenever you say that, I go as hard as a rock."

Her hand fumbled behind her to stroke his cock. "Good."

Under her brief caress, he closed his eyes.

"Should I move?" she asked.

"No." His voice was muffled in her hair. "We can manage like this."

He pushed down the top of her shift so he could caress her bare breast. He teased the nipple until she was gasping and bumping against him. "Oh, Brock."

His hand strayed to her hip where he scrunched her shift up, until he could work his way under it to cup her mound. He stroked her cleft until she was wet and ready, and her breath emerged in erratic gasps.

"Part your legs and tilt back toward me." Arousal roughened his voice.

She obeyed with an alacrity that fired his excitement. He caught her thigh and lifted it to give him access. He slid into her with a slick ease that shuddered through him like an earthquake. She whimpered with pleasure and pushed back, taking him deeper.

He paused, drinking in the wonder. The snug clasp of her muscles, the scent of jasmine and aroused woman that enveloped him, the slippery silk of her hair against his face. He burrowed into the cloud of hair until he kissed her nape. She trembled and released a long sigh. He skimmed his teeth across the skin and ended with a gentle bite.

"Oh!" When she tightened, heat blasted him. He started to move in leisurely thrusts, going as deep as he could and lingering at the end of each incursion.

"Brock, that's...that's wonderful," she murmured, placing her hand over his where he held her thigh.

"Tell me," he said in a low growl. There was something incomparably exciting about Selina saying naughty things in that precise contralto.

"Tell you?"

"Aye."

"I can hardly think when you're inside me. Now you want me to talk?"

"I love to fuck you. I want to hear how you feel when I do."

When she shifted, the movement threatened to blast his head off. Then she began to speak. "Your...organ..."

"Cock," he said on a groan.

She made an incoherent sound in her throat. "Your...cock is so big, I feel like you fill every inch inside me. I love it when you move. When you go fast, you make me dizzy with excitement. When you go slowly..."

He suited his actions to her words, pulling back with a gradual retreat that left her gasping.

"...I feel like we become one person. I feel like you appreciate me the way nobody ever has before. I feel like what we do extends out into...eternity."

Dear God, be careful what you wish for.

When she'd started talking, it had been a game, a spice to flavor his arousal. He should have known that she'd propel him far beyond that. He'd passed his thirty years in the shallows, but Selina drew him out into dangerous depths of emotion.

His wicked heart cramped as he slid into her, glorying in her welcome. He rocked his hips in a gentle rhythm. "Selina..."

"I can't..." Her hand tightened over his, and her voice thickened.

"I love your quim," he said hoarsely, as he set up a slow, sure movement. If only to justify those beautiful words, he wanted to pleasure her forever.

To his surprise, an exhalation of amusement escaped her. "My quim loves you back."

He groaned. "How the hell can I resist you?"

He reached down to tangle his fingers in the silky curls covering her mound. They were damp and soft, and the way she shifted under every thrust built his arousal. Each time he buried his length inside her, she sighed with delight. Those gentle moans played sweet music in his ears.

With a sublime lack of striving, she tipped over into a lavish climax. His balls tightened with the urge to lose himself, but he kept up the slow, intense momentum as long as he could. When she climaxed again on a soft cry of satisfaction, he struggled to hold himself in. Even as she came down off the heights, he slid his hand down her stomach and between her legs to toy with her clitoris. She convulsed around him and cried out once more.

On one last languorous glide, he pulled free and insinuated his cock between her thighs. He groaned with pleasure as he spilled on her skin while she still shook in ecstasy. Jerking against her back, he buried his face in that glorious fall of hair.

She reached down between her legs to caress the sensitive head of his dick. Her touch was tender. "That was lovely," she said in a choked voice.

"Aye, it was." He shifted to leave the bed and fetch a flannel, but she made a soft protest.

"Not yet."

He slumped against her back and slid his arms around her, drawing her into his chest. His hand shaped the soft weight of her breast. "Not yet."

They drowsed in the afterglow. It felt like much later when she spoke in a whisper. "I use my hands on myself."

"Hmm?"

She continued in an even lower voice, so he had to press closer to hear. "You asked...you asked how someone who had never found satisfaction in a man's arms knows what pleasure means."

Surprise rippled through him, although he wasn't as shocked as he might have been. This was the obvious answer. He'd been a fool to doubt what she'd told him about her husband. From their first kiss, he'd noted that she was unused to enjoying a man's touch.

"I'm glad."

He was. He couldn't imagine the demure woman he'd first met daring to explore her body, however unfulfilling her husband's attentions. But the lover who had taken him to paradise over and over through this exceptional day, that woman had the courage to seek what marriage denied her.

"You are?" He heard sleepy disbelief in the question.

"Aye, with all my heart."

She rested her hand over where he clasped her breast. He was close to asleep when she spoke again. "Since the first moment I saw you, the lover in my mind when I touch myself is you."

Her honesty sliced into his heart with the precision of a surgeon's scalpel. "My darling, I don't deserve you," he murmured.

He kissed the point of her shoulder, bared where her shift slipped down her arm. Her skin tasted of salt and Selina.

Another long pause while he basked in having this miracle of a woman lying in his arms. Then she went on, and the aching sadness in her words had him closing his eyes in an agony of regret.

"From now on, whenever I find my pleasure, I'll always picture you."

So often she'd stolen his ability to speak. Now his throat closed on more of those words he couldn't allow himself to say. He bundled her tight against him and told himself he could bear to part with her when the time came. But he knew himself to be a liar.

CHAPTER NINE

"**I** can hear it ahead of us, but I can't see it," Selina said breathlessly, as she gripped Brock's hand and stumbled after him along the frozen path.

Around her towered tall winter-brown reeds. Snow squeaked underfoot. It had snowed ever since the night she'd arrived in Essex. Now, on the day before she was due to go back to London, the weather cleared enough for her and Brock to leave the house.

With a determination that grew more and more tattered, she pushed aside thoughts of tomorrow's parting. She refused to spoil these last hours with her lover with bitter regret that this was all she would have.

He strode ahead of her, bundled up in a greatcoat and a thick woolen scarf, and with his hat pulled down low over his ears. It was perishingly cold.

"It's not far, trust me," he said, glancing back with brilliant green eyes.

She'd wondered if a week in his company would blunt the impact of his extraordinary looks. If anything, his handsomeness had a more powerful effect on her now than when she'd first seen him at Derwent Hall. And when she'd first seen him, his flashing dark beauty had made her knees tremble and her heart race.

They followed a narrow hunters' track through reed beds which rustled in the wind. The sound was eerie, like a thousand voices whispering at her.

She gulped in a deep breath of salt-laden air and summoned up a smile. "I do trust you."

His gaze softened, and he drew her forward for a quick kiss. The heat that filled her as his lips moved over hers made a mockery of the freezing air.

"What was that for?" she asked shakily, after he pulled away and plowed on.

"For pleasure. And because you trust me. And because I can."

And because the wretched truth was that after tomorrow, he'd never kiss her again.

No, don't think about that.

"I wish you could come back here in autumn. The marshes are alive with life. We could take a boat and go exploring."

She squeezed his gloved hand. "That would be lovely."

But never to be. Never was the saddest word she knew.

No, don't think about that either.

She'd struggled so hard to cling to their every minute together, striving to stretch each second into an hour. But in the way of time, the seconds had turned into hours had turned into days. Now only one night remained. Selina didn't know how she could bear it.

The rolling thunder ahead of her wasn't loud enough to overpower the keening sorrow in her heart. They turned a bend on the path, and a gap opened up in the reeds. Something huge and gray sparkled in the space.

A few more steps and the reeds ended. She and Brock stood on a sandy knoll above an empty stretch of silvery sand.

"Oh, Brock..." Tears rose to her eyes, as she surveyed the vast magnificence of the North Sea. The water spread in shining immensity all the way to the faraway horizon.

As she leaned into him, he curled his arm around her. Warmth radiated out from him to ease her heart, even as a sharp breeze, stronger here in the open, whipped around her cheeks. She wore one of his coats, and she'd wrapped a thick shawl around her head.

"I'm a man of my word. Our first day, I promised that I'd show you the sea."

She'd learned he was a man of his word, despite the world calling him so wicked. He was also kind and even-tempered, not to mention a breathtakingly skillful lover. She'd expected only the last when she accepted his invitation to share his bed. It turned out that he was so much more than she'd anticipated. Interesting and clever and imaginative. And his dry humor had her laughing more often than she'd ever laughed in her life.

She'd miss the lover the way she'd miss an amputated leg. But she'd miss the man even worse.

No, don't think about that.

Brock shifted to stand behind Selina, wrapping her in his arms to shelter her from the wind. She nestled against his chest. This reminded her of the way they often slept, with him curled up against her back. As she felt then, she felt now. Protected and cherished.

She blinked away more futile tears and made herself drink in the spectacular view. In the distance, the clouds broke and the water turned dazzling silver.

"All my life, I've wanted to see the sea," she said in a thick voice. "I'm so glad that I saw it with you."

"You'll never forget it," he murmured, resting his chin on her head and folding his arms around her even more securely.

"No," she said on a mere whisper of sound, and the answer encompassed everything that had happened in these remarkable days.

Brock noticed that just as on their arrival at the hunting lodge, neither Selina nor he did justice to Mary's cooking. Which was a pity as his kinswoman had worked hard to make his last dinner with Selina special. But the roast pheasant and the extravagant spun-sugar dessert returned to the kitchen mostly untouched.

Since their first night here, when he'd been in such a lather to claim Selina, he'd managed to claw back a shred of civilized behavior. Most nights, he joined her in the drawing room for a brandy or a port before he bustled her upstairs. His impatience to have her under him hadn't lessened any, but he'd learned to rein his need in. At least for an hour or so. Although during their stay in Essex, the Earl of Bruard and his mistress were in the habit of retiring notably early.

Now he surveyed that mistress across the damask tablecloth. This last week, he'd come to know her so well. He knew the sounds she made when she found her peak, he knew the soft hum of delight she gave when he kissed her. He knew the surprised gurgle of her laughter, as if amusement took her unawares. He knew how she hungered for him, because even after a week of debauchery, she stared at him as if she wanted to gobble him up in one bite.

But tonight as he studied her, he realized that she remained as mysterious and untamable as the sea she'd so loved seeing this afternoon. A lifetime together wouldn't be time enough to reveal all this glorious woman's secrets.

He had mere hours until they must part forever.

It was a damnable tragedy.

"Shall we take a brandy in the next room?"

She set aside the half-empty wineglass she'd been toying with and raised fathomless brown eyes to his. For this, their last evening together, she wore her best gown and her magnificent hair was caught up in a mass of curls. The coiffure was lovely, although its principal effect on him was the temptation to dismantle it.

He'd always thought Selina beautiful, but a week of sensual fulfillment had turned her into the loveliest woman he'd ever seen. Her creamy skin glowed, and her lips were soft and full as if she'd only just left off kissing him. Sensual awareness weighted her every movement.

"No, let's go upstairs," she murmured. "I want to be in your arms."

"That's what I want, too," he said soberly, rising to pull out her chair for her. "Do you want to race me again?"

She laughed as she stood, although he could tell that it was an effort. Dinner had been a quiet meal. They both felt the crushing weight of tomorrow's goodbyes looming ahead. "Not tonight."

"Then allow me to escort you, my lady," he said, presenting his arm.

As she curled her fingers around his elbow, her smile was wistful. Her touch was warm, even through the layers of his coat and shirt. From the start, he'd been preternaturally aware of her. He'd wondered if familiarity would dull his urgent reaction, but she just needed to look at him sideways to make him as hard as iron.

"We only have to make it to the bedroom." Selina gave him a conspiratorial smile and one of those slanting glances under gold-tipped lashes that drove him wild. As if he wasn't wild enough for her already.

"You know I'm ready for you?" he asked in surprise.

The smile that curved that lush red mouth turned smug. "Of course I know."

"Of course you do," he echoed.

No lover had ever been so attuned to him. It was one of the many reasons why the world exploded into a blinding fireball when they came together.

They left the dining room and crossed the shadowy hall to the staircase. As he mounted each step, he was achingly aware that this was the last time he and Selina would retire to bed together.

Brock beat back the thought because it was too painful to face. But a universe of repressed feeling deepened his voice as he pushed open the door to the chamber. "I don't want to sleep a wink tonight, my darling."

She watched him with that serious, covetous gaze that only made him want her more. "Let's see in the dawn."

With a self-confident sway of her hips that would have been foreign to the woman he first met, she moved past. He couldn't bear to think of her going back to that demure lady, not when he'd watched her blossom into this vivid creature. But he supposed she must, damn it.

He followed her inside, confused, troubled, unhappy. Randy as hell.

Because he suffered such unfamiliar emotional turmoil, she caught him by surprise when she turned and flung herself against him in a flurry of blue silk.

"Selina?" he gasped, as she fumbled behind him and slammed the door shut.

"Shh, don't talk," she said in an intense voice he'd never heard before. She sounded like she wasn't far off crying. "Tonight, I just want to feel. Because I'll never feel like this again in my whole life."

"You…"

"No, for pity's sake, don't say anything," she hissed and caught his head between shaking hands to drag him down for a kiss, clumsy with violent emotion.

He kissed her back with all the hunger she ignited in him. The kiss held no finesse or tenderness. When at last she drew away, his chest was heaving.

With a hint of apology, Brock touched her lip. "I bruised you."

"I don't care," she muttered, eyes brilliant with excitement and something that looked like despair.

He reached out to offer her comfort. "Let me…"

She placed her hands flat on his chest and pushed him back until he hit the door. "No! No more talk."

He didn't resist. During these last days, he'd shared her passion over and over. She'd offered him a satisfaction he'd never found before, but the edge to her demands tonight threatened to burn him to ash.

Selina dropped to her knees in front of him. Her skirts pooled around her like a patch of summer sky.

She tugged so roughly at the fastenings on his trousers that a button flew off to bounce across the carpet.

"What the devil…"

He caught her face in one hand and tipped it up until she met his eyes. His dick was thick and throbbing after that fierce kiss and the brush of her eager hands across his clothing. The ferocious concentration she devoted to undressing him heightened his arousal. "You want me in your mouth?"

"Yes," she said on a long exhalation.

They'd tried this variation a couple of times. At first, she'd been uncertain if willing, but in the end, as he'd come to expect, she'd lifted him to summits he'd never before approached. He, the famous rake, completely undone by the virtuous widow.

"I'd like that."

She was breathing in broken gasps. Standing over her, he had a superb view of the way her breasts rose and fell under the modest bodice. "This time I want you to stay until the end."

Shock and sinful anticipation slammed through him. His cock twitched in fervent agreement with her suggestion. She'd told him not to speak. She achieved her goal. Her boldness stole his ability to put two words together. He'd never yet come in her mouth, fearing she'd find the act revolting.

Now he stared down into her flushed face with its bright, yearning eyes and asked himself how he'd ever reached that conclusion. Hadn't this woman proven herself his equal in daring over and over?

He swallowed, but it didn't help to ease the tightness of his throat. "I…"

She sent him a seductive smile, composed of delight in his flabbergasted reaction and anticipation over what she was about to do.

Selina caught his hand and lifted it from her cheek. "I want this."

He gulped for air again, then altogether lost the ability to breathe as she kissed his palm, circling the center with her tongue. A jolt of heat made him stagger. An even stronger reaction crashed through him when she took his thumb into her mouth and sucked. As she drew on him, he couldn't help imagining her devoting the same attention to his prick.

He groaned and sagged against the door. "I'm all yours," he grated out.

The stark reality was that was nothing but the truth.

Through dazed eyes, he watched her undo his trousers with hands that had regained their deftness. When she uncovered his erect cock, a choked murmur of admiration escaped her.

With a tenderness that threatened to blast him to dust, she took his throbbing member in her hand. Lost to her touch, he closed his eyes and rested his head back on the wood panels behind him. He ground his teeth and told himself he wouldn't come. But as she started to stroke him, that resolution became more and more difficult to keep.

Her caresses became more purposeful, and he clenched his hands at his sides as he struggled for control. When she rubbed her thumb over the drop of moisture on the tip, his breath released in a hiss that expressed pleasure and frustration.

Brock jerked when she closed her mouth over him. The warm, wet suction was familiar, but it never failed to set his blood on fire. One hand caressed his tight balls, while the other curved around to squeeze his buttocks and press him closer to that brazen, sumptuous mouth.

She began to suck and use her tongue on him. He was so close to losing himself, it was a miracle he didn't flood her mouth there and then. With another guttural groan, he buried his shaking hands in her hair. "God Almighty, Selina, what you do to me."

Her hand circled the base of his dick with a firm grip. How did she know to the fraction of an inch how he liked it? She began to move her head in an infernal imitation of the way he thrust inside her.

But this time, praise all the angels, if angels could bring themselves to contemplate such lewdness, he didn't have to pull free. He could give himself to her in a way he never had before. The prospect made his head reel, even as the dark flow of arousal swept him away.

She moved faster now, increasing the pressure. He groaned again and pushed further into her mouth. He was so close, so damned close.

With a muffled sound of excitement, she took him deeper. She squeezed the base of his dick, then fondled his aching bollocks.

It was all over for his restraint. On a cracked groan, he clutched her skull hard between shaking hands and began to pump into her mouth. Somewhere through the wild storm, he expected her to pull back. But she took all he gave. When at last she lifted her head to gaze up at him, he watched her delicate throat move as she swallowed.

Her eyes were as dark as night and heavy with female satisfaction. With a luxuriant lack of shame, she lifted her hand from him with a final caress. She wiped the mouth that glistened with his seed.

His knees threatened to collapse under him. Gratitude cramped his overflowing heart.

"Och, lassie, you're such a bonny woman," he said, lapsing into the Scots of his childhood as he so rarely did.

"I liked it," she said in a hoarse whisper. "I felt like you were mine."

He grimaced with the force of his emotions. "I'm yours anyway."

Clumsily he hauled her to her feet and kissed her. She twined herself around him as if she couldn't get close enough. When they drew apart, they were both breathless.

"That you would do that for me..." Coherence remained too much to ask. He straightened away from the door, unsure his legs would support him. His blood ran sluggish with the lingering effects of his mighty climax in her mouth.

She smiled. Her hair was a wild tangle and threatened to tumble free of its pins. Her eyes glowed with excitement. "I did it for myself, too. You've given me such pleasure, I love that I can return the favor."

"You give me pleasure just by breathing," he said in a voice gruff with feeling. And because she'd been so endlessly generous, he dared to make a last forbidden request. "But there's one more thing I'd like."

Faint bewilderment drew her brows together, but her answer reflected the trust they'd built up during these days of searing intimacy. "Anything."

Despite her quick cooperation, he wasn't sure she'd take this next step, although she'd make him a happy man if she did. He took her hand and drew her into the center of the room. "Ever since our first night, I've wanted this."

She'd stopped looking uncertain. Instead she looked intrigued. "Oh?"

Encouraged, he went on. "I want to watch you touch yourself."

Embarrassment and guilty excitement seized Selina. "You want to watch?"

He gave a sharp nod, as his eyes burned into hers. "You said you thought of me when you touched yourself. I want to see you do it. So I can imagine you doing it again, when you..."

Leave.

"I'll feel so awkward."

His expression darkened. "Will you do it for me? It would give me something to hold onto."

How could she deny him? She read the yearning in his face even as she asked, "You really want this?"

He nodded again. "More than I can say."

"Very well," she said in a reedy voice.

Without shifting his eyes from her, he reached out to grab a chair. He sank into it, stretching his long legs out before him. If she hadn't read the bristling tension in his straight shoulders and the adamant set of his jaw, she might almost imagine he treated this moment as unimportant. She supposed that he was trying to set her at ease.

Not much chance of that.

During a week when they'd spent hours naked together, she'd become used to his eyes on her unclothed body. But this was different. This felt like a performance.

She hesitated and shot him a questioning glance as her courage faltered. He smiled with the singular sweetness that always made her heart expand, until it threatened to break free of her chest.

"Selina, if you don't want to do this, it's all right."

She straightened her spine. What would this hurt her? She'd do anything to give Brock pleasure. Yet her knees trembled as she stepped forward and turned her back. "Will you unlace me? If I'd realized what you wanted me to do tonight, I'd have chosen another dress."

His soft chuckle held a wealth of male contentment. The chair gave a soft creak as he stood. "I should have warned you."

"I'm rather glad you didn't. It would have spoiled my dinner."

She felt him begin to work on her laces. "You didn't eat much anyway."

"Neither did you."

"No."

A silence descended as he finished undoing her dress. Very gently, he turned her around and kissed her with the same sweetness she'd seen in his smile.

Selina sighed and blinked away the mist that persisted in settling in front of her eyes. She clung to his shirt until she was sure she wouldn't collapse in a heap. After a week of kisses, she should be inured to the way the touch of his lips turned her world topsy-turvy.

"Now show me," he whispered, sitting down again.

On tottering legs, Selina returned to the center of the room. His eyes were avid as she lifted her arms to remove the few pins that held her hair up off her neck. When she'd taken Brock in her mouth, he'd buried his hands in her hair as he surrendered to that paroxysm of pleasure.

When he'd spurted into her mouth, she'd felt so brave and powerful. She needed to wrench some of that bravery back now.

She reached down deep inside herself. If this was how Brock meant to remember her, she wanted him to think of her as strong and resolute. A woman proud of everything she'd done during this unforgettable week with her dissolute lover.

So while nerves urged her to rush, she made each movement slow and deliberate. As she unpeeled her dress from her shoulders and down her arms, urgency tightened Brock's face.

"Oh, yes," he breathed, leaning forward. His air of relaxation vanished.

Selina found it in her to tease him, holding the dress to her breasts for an instant before slipping it down over her hips until it crumpled to the floor. She stepped out of it and began to unhook her corset.

By the time her corset parted to reveal her transparent shift, he was breathing audibly and his long-fingered hands clenched the carved arms of the chair. She couldn't mistake his excitement. He'd fastened his trousers since she'd serviced him on her knees. Now his erect cock tented the material.

"Don't stop, for pity's sake," he croaked out.

This gradual revelation of her body to her eager lover excited her, too. With a languid grace she'd never imagined herself capable of, she slipped her corset off so her breasts bobbed loose against her shift. Beneath the drift of her petticoats, she was wet and throbbing. She rubbed her thighs together to feed her craving.

This wasn't at all like what she did in the lonely space of her bedroom. There every action was furtive and poisoned by shame. Brock's unconcealed appreciation made her feel like a queen.

But the game they played caught her in its talons just as tight as it caught him. She couldn't bear to stop now. His eyes focused on the swell of her bosom. She always touched her nipples when she sought satisfaction, but never before with such lascivious pleasure.

She cupped her breasts, holding them up for Brock's hot gaze. Through the fine material, she plucked at her nipples. She was so close to the edge that the sensation tugged at her womb and an involuntary cry escaped her.

"Hell, Selina, you're going to kill me," he groaned.

She slid one hand down her chest and fondled her breast under the shift. Then with increasing urgency, she pushed away the fabric so she presented herself to him.

"Touch them," he grated out, his hand covering his member. His face was flushed, and a muscle jerked in his lean cheek.

Selina adored that she could do this to him. When she'd first seen him, he'd seemed a man apart, untouched by messy human emotion. Now she turned him into this shaking, desperate lover who was on the brink of losing control at the sight of her body.

She closed her eyes and concentrated on arousing herself. Squeezing her nipples. Fondling her breasts. Teasing herself until she was shaking.

When her nipples were tight and aching, she reached down to untie her petticoats. She'd like to continue to titillate Brock, but she verged too close. She pressed her hand over her mound to find some relief. It wasn't enough. With swift eagerness, she stripped her shift away, so she was naked. She hadn't worn drawers since she'd arrived at the hunting lodge.

Brock inhaled great lungfuls of air, and the hand he placed over his erection moved with increasing speed.

"What...what do you do once you're naked?" he asked in a choked voice.

She backed toward the bed. "I...I use my hand."

Her knees felt like wet wool, and she tumbled back onto the mattress. Her touch on her body excited her, but more than that, Brock's unabashed enjoyment built her responses beyond anything she'd achieved on her own.

"Show me."

Shyness was long forgotten. Her insides tightened with the irresistible drive to climax. She shifted to give him a clear view of her sex and how she stroked herself.

She raised her knees and began to explore the drenched folds of her quim. The air was thick with the scent of her need, musky and salty and hot. She found the place where her pleasure focused and played with it, until a violent convulsion of bliss shuddered through her. She cried out as every muscle in her body clenched in rapture.

She opened dazed eyes to see Brock stroking his length through his gaping trousers. His lips were full, and his eyes were half-closed in sensual delight.

She was so lost in what she'd just done to herself that she barely noticed when he surged to his feet. He paused near the bed to strip away his clothes in a careless rush that betrayed his frenzy.

"You're the most exciting woman I've ever known," he said in a guttural voice.

She gave him a weary smile as he kneeled naked above her and without any preliminaries plunged into her full-length. Straightaway she toppled over into another climax. Better this time because he was with her.

"Oh, yes," she gasped as he moved inside her, seeming to penetrate so deep, he reached her very heart.

She dug her fingers into the hard muscles of his back, feeling the way they flexed with every thrust. She crossed her legs over his buttocks, angling up to take more of him. She felt his crisis approaching, and this time, she couldn't bear to exile him to his effortful, lonely relief.

"Stay," she forced out.

Not sure he'd heard her aright, Brock went stock still. He raised his head so he could see her face. "Selina?"

She brought him down for a desperate kiss, even as her body gripped him tighter. He was so close, he nearly spilled.

"It's our last night, Brock. I want all of you."

Blazing excitement crashed through him. The idea of giving Selina everything he had was intoxicating.

He stared into deep brown eyes that glowed with some profound emotion he couldn't put a name to. "Are you sure?"

Her lips lengthened in a smile that threatened to break his heart. "I want to know how it feels when you give yourself to me. I want to remember when we were truly one."

Even through his physical extremity, her bravery and her vulnerability touched his black soul. "Selina, you humble me," he said in a voice that cracked.

He bent his head, and she greeted him with another of those earth-shattering kisses. Curse it, he'd planned to spend days on end kissing her. Now they came to their last few hours, and he realized that he hadn't kissed her nearly enough.

A lifetime wouldn't be enough.

"Come inside me, Brock. I want to take that away with me."

He knew what a concession she made with that request. Within little more than a week, she'd share Cecil's bed. When she asked this of him, she gave Brock her ultimate loyalty.

He'd promised her joy, but compared to what she'd given him in return, that was an insignificant gift. She turned him into a man he didn't recognize. A better, wiser, more principled man.

"Selina, I may leave you with child." He hated that his conscience, so quiet through his adult life, awoke now.

"I'd love that," she said fervently.

"But if the child looks like me..."

"I'd love that, too."

He frowned, even as his unruly appetites urged him to accept her offer before she thought better of it. Most of his life, he'd been at the mercy of those appetites. Selina tugged on his desire more than any other woman ever had. But she also called on his heart and mind in a way unheralded in his reckless, selfish existence. "What about Cecil?"

Tears glittered in her eyes, and she bucked her hips toward him with an insistence that smashed through him like cannon fire. "Don't talk about Cecil." Her voice broke as she went on. "In fact, don't talk at all, damn you."

He couldn't help settling deeper into her body. The effort of holding back became agonizing. "But you..."

Eyes bright with tears bored into his, as though she struggled to drill all the way to his soul. If she did manage to catch a glimpse of that unimpressive entity, she'd find her own reflection looking back at her. "Please, Brock. Please."

Knowing it was wrong, knowing he might cause her untold damage – Cecil wouldn't take kindly to a cuckoo in his nest – Brock couldn't resist her pleading. Nor could he resist the prospect of giving himself to her in the most profound way he knew.

After a brief, hard kiss, he began to move once more. It wasn't long before his crisis built, flooding his head with dark heat. The rush started at the soles of his feet and flowed up his legs and focused on his aching balls.

Brock lifted his head from where he'd buried it in her shoulder. He needed to see Selina's face when he gave himself into her keeping as he never had before.

She looked strained and on edge. Her eyes were heavy with the rise of her own climax, and her lips were satiny and full, parted to allow him a glimpse of her small white teeth.

He shifted again and watched her expression change to triumph as she crossed the barrier into feminine ecstasy. Then thought deserted him entirely. His muscles contracted in a wild spasm, and his seed spurted into her womb.

She cried out and dug her fingernails into his shoulders. The sting became yet another part of the incandescence. He moved over her, until he'd given her every ounce of the man he was.

It had been a week of unsurpassed pleasure. But nothing had prepared him for this blazing union when Selina became his blood and his bone and his flesh. She might leave him in the morning, but somewhere in eternity, they were united forever.

As he slumped over her in a haze of satiation he'd never felt before, she wrapped her arms around him. "Thank you, Brock," she said in a choked voice.

CHAPTER TEN

Selina stirred from a restless doze with a premonition of looming disaster. She was sprawled across Brock, one arm crooked on his chest and her leg flung over his. It was as if even lost in oblivion, she couldn't bear the idea of letting him go.

"Oh, no," she gasped.

With a gentle hand, Brock smoothed the tangled hair away from her face. "What's wrong?"

She jerked away to sit up and stare down at him in horror. "I went to sleep."

The fire had burned low and the candles guttered, but there was enough light for her to see his tender smile. "You were tired."

She'd been silly with exhaustion. After that unprecedented moment when he'd filled her with his seed and she felt like the world exploded in a conflagration of light, they'd lain together in perfect communion, only talking now and again. Accepting his essence into her body had been a transcendent experience, one she'd treasure as long as she lived.

After a while, he'd begun to touch her, giving her another climax with his hand. She'd used her mouth on him again. That time, he lost himself between her breasts. Then, plague take her, she'd fallen asleep.

"But I don't want to waste a moment." A horrid fear twisted her stomach. "Is it time for us to go?"

With a late sunrise and the curtains drawn, it was impossible to know how late it was. If she frittered away her last minutes at this house in sleep, she'd never forgive herself.

Rolling over, he lifted his pocket watch from the bedside table. He clicked it open and angled it toward the fire so he could see the dial. "No, it's not five yet."

Two hours until they were due to leave, then. It wasn't much of a reprieve. Selina had to reach London tonight, so they needed to be on the road before dawn. She couldn't bring herself to contemplate the thought.

With a sleepy sigh, Brock set his watch back on the table and turned to curve his hand behind her neck. "Come here."

The low purr and the sensual gleam in his eyes told her he had plans for what time remained to them. She had no objection. How could she refuse one last chance to experience that radiant closeness?

The taste of his lips was delicious. The kiss soon turned carnal, and Brock crushed her into the sheets. She reached down to encircle his erection, and a growl of pleasure escaped her. "I don't know how you do it. We've been going all night."

He caught her hand and drew it to his lips. "You're all the incentive I need, my bonny."

She wriggled until she cradled him between her thighs. "Then don't wait. I need to fuck."

His laugh was wry. "You'd better forget I taught you such dirty words."

As she bent her knees on either side of his narrow hips, she regarded him without smiling. "I never want to forget a single second of what we've done together."

His amusement faded, and she saw that he was doing his best to place a brave face on their forthcoming separation. The prospect of imminent parting left him devastated, too. She should feel better to know that this affair had branded him, but she was too heartsick.

"Selina..." He kissed her again, a turbulent expression of desire and regret that had her heart cramping with poignant emotion.

She ripped her lips away from his and gazed into his face. The first time she saw him, she'd noticed his striking beauty. Now she saw so much more. Kindness and humor and intelligence. And care.

She wondered what Brock would look like when he was old. If he persisted in this life of idle debauchery, it would mark him. The cynicism he shed in her company would set a permanent sneer into his features. Whereas if he found purpose and happiness, his beauty would endure.

I could make you happy.

Selina capped that thought before it drove her to despair. Wishing for what she couldn't have was the sure path to madness.

"Put your cock inside me," she whispered, despite everything a little shocked at such words leaving her lips.

He smiled down at her with the affection that she'd tried so hard not to rely upon. Because while he might be fond of her, she had no delusion that this affair would change his life. Once she was gone, he'd take another woman into his bed, then another. And despite her strictures to herself that jealousy did her no good, right now she was sick with jealousy. She wanted to hunt down those unknown hussies and rip every hair from their no doubt empty heads.

She supposed she'd hear about his new amours. The papers were quick to print any gossip about the disreputable Lord Bruard and his scandalous exploits.

Every time she saw his name, her heart would break all over again.

But that was in the future. A future that seemed as bleak and empty as a desert. At this moment, she had the man she wanted in her arms and he desired only her. She refused to let bitterness infect their last hours.

"Aye, with pleasure, my sweet lassie." His brogue was thicker this morning. Always a sign of strong emotion.

Reveling in the perfect union, she rose to meet him as he slid inside her. She'd spend the rest of her life feeling as though half of her soul was missing.

Brock propped himself up on his elbows and stared down into her face with intent green eyes. He set up a slow, relentless rhythm, penetrating to the hilt, before withdrawing in a smooth glide that made her quake. She reached her peak twice while he kept up that incessant rocking motion. With every thrust, he laid claim to her.

They didn't speak. Their bodies said everything they needed to.

Only toward the end when Brock's chest was heaving and his skin was damp with the effort of holding back did a guttural question escape him. "Shall I pull out?"

She firmed her grip on his hips and drew him closer. "No."

Even then, the deep strokes continued, until Selina shattered into another exhausted climax. She was swollen and aching after all these hours of passion, but this final consummation was sweeter than honey. Sweeter yet was the moment he went still and groaned in release.

When it was over, he stretched out behind her, holding her in a loose embrace, as they'd lain so often in this bed. She blinked back acid tears and placed her hand over his where it caressed one bare breast. "You've given me joy, Brock. Such joy. Just as you promised."

She waited for him to respond, but with a broken sigh, he buried his face in her disheveled hair. His hold tightened, and they lay in silence as their last minutes together ticked away.

Brock glanced out the carriage window. "We're not far from the Blue Wagon."

Yesterday's break in the weather hadn't lasted. The sky lowered heavy and gray, and sleet flew in the biting wind. The coachman would be as cold as an icicle and must curse his master for making him drive on such a bitter day.

So far, the roads had remained firm, frozen after the snow, but Selina knew the trip back to London would turn into a muddy nightmare. Even now, the coach showed a dangerous tendency to skid, and they were more than an hour behind the time she said she'd reach the Blue Wagon.

Selina sat up from where she leaned against Brock's shoulder and smoothed her hair. Compared to the journey to the marshes, this trip had been uneventful. There had been no breathtaking sensual encounters. There hadn't even been much conversation. Selina couldn't bear to put the profound experiences of the last week into words, and the idea of discussing forthcoming plans made her feel ill. So she'd rested against Brock, trying to draw strength from the warmth of his arm around her.

He shifted across to the opposite seat. "Your carriage will be waiting?"

He'd asked her this already. She supposed there was some satisfaction in knowing he was also on edge about their imminent parting. "I hope so. I assume Kitty will be there, too."

"Gerald comes home from school tomorrow morning."

"Yes."

"That will be nice."

"Yes. Although it's going to be a busy week."

Brock looked discontented and folded his arms over his chest as he kicked the base of his seat. "Because of the wedding."

"Yes."

The atmosphere between them turned thorny, although what else could she say? They both knew that in a few days, duty necessitated that she became Mrs. Cecil Canley-Smythe. As she drew on her gloves, her hands shook. In her private dictionary, duty had become a synonym for desolation.

Brock went back to staring moodily out the window. After a while, he released a deep sigh and directed his attention to her. "Don't go back to him, Selina."

Shock struck her motionless. A silence crashed down between them, filled only with the creak of the carriage and the thud of the horses' hooves.

She struggled to summon a response. "But you know that I..."

One elegant hand sliced the air. Brock was pale, and his jaw was set like iron. The green eyes glittered with furious determination. "Stay with me."

Brock, why are you torturing us both like this? It was difficult enough sticking to her purpose, without having cruel temptation thrown before her.

Her hands clenched in her olive green skirts. "You know that's impossible."

"Why?"

What was his game? It seemed almost spiteful that he brought this up now. Because he must guess how it tore her apart to leave him. He knew all about women, and she'd done very little to hide her feelings.

So anger edged her tone when she replied. "I have Gerald to consider. I can't become your mistress. I can't tar his future with scandal." Her voice softened. "It would be different if I just had myself to worry about. I'd stay with you and dare the world to despise me. Any price I paid would be worthwhile."

"Is that true?" He looked startled. "You'd give up everything in return for no guarantees?"

Her lips turned down. "I'd gain more than I ever lost. My good reputation has been a cold companion. You, on the other hand, make me feel as if I live every minute to the fullest."

He leaned forward to seize her hands with an eager desperation that threatened to break her heart. Who knew that a heart could break over and over? Each time the wound cut deeper. How in heaven's name was she going to survive the years ahead? The thought of Gerald had kept her strong for so long, but even her stalwart love for her son quailed at the barren existence stretching before her.

"You would give me that?"

"Gladly." She gripped his hands hard. "But there's Gerald. You can't ask me to put what we have above what I owe my son."

"I don't." He paused. "But hearing those words is something I'll always treasure."

She blinked back idiotic, useless tears. "So you must see why I can't stay with you."

His expression remained intent. Over the creak of the carriage, she heard distant shouting, but it couldn't penetrate the fraught atmosphere inside the vehicle.

"I honor your devotion to your son." She knew he must think back to his own mother. The shouts outside grew louder. "But you're a woman as well as a mother. What about you and what you need?"

Feeling stupid, she stared at Brock. "I..."

The sentence ended in a sharp cry, as the carriage slewed to the left. Battling to keep her place on the seat, she heard confused yelling, the screams of frightened horses, and the crack of the whip.

"What the devil!" Brock surged forward to wrap her in his arms so when the coach swerved again and tilted onto its side, she smashed against him and not unforgiving wood.

"Brock?" she screamed, as the world turned topsy-turvy. Her ears rang with the crack of shattering wood.

His body was the one solid thing remaining. She clutched at him, as the carriage tipped even further and came to rest at a drunken angle.

When she caught her breath enough to open her eyes, she and Brock were huddled against the door. Broken glass showered them. Outside, it sounded like utter chaos reigned. Angry voices and neighing horses.

Brock's embrace tightened. "For God's sake, Selina, are you all right?"

"Yes, I think so. Are you?" She raised her head and through her dizziness, she saw that his face was stark with worry as he stared down at her. "You're bleeding."

From under his disordered black hair, blood trickled down his forehead. "Am I?"

Dear God, let him be all right. Let him not be hurt.

Her shaking hand touched the sticky wetness. His quick thinking had saved her from injury. But she couldn't bear to think that in protecting her, he'd sustained serious harm. "Does it hurt anywhere else?"

"I'm damned uncomfortable, but I think I'm fine. Some of the window glass must have caught me. I'm sure it's just a scratch."

"Head wounds can be dangerous. Did you black out? Any double vision?"

The carriage lurched and settled further on its side, pitching Brock and Selina harder against the door which creaked in protest. She dared a glance out the shattered window and saw a muddy ditch below them. Her stomach dipped with vertigo.

Before she could right herself, the door on the other side slammed open and a stranger wearing a thick greatcoat stared down at them. "Are you hurt, maister, mistress?"

"Nothing serious," Brock said with admirable coolness. "What happened?"

"You were coming toward me, when you hit a patch of black ice and slid right across in front of my team. God's blood, I thought we were all a goner."

"Is Erskine safe?" Brock asked.

"If that's your coachman, sir, I do believe he's broken his arm. He was thrown clear in the accident."

"Bugger," Brock muttered. "Poor sod. What about the horses?"

"Better news there. I've released them. They're frightened, but no injuries."

"That's something."

"Can I help you out of there?"

"Aye, please. Take the lady first." Brock bent his head to speak into Selina's ear. "Can you move, sweetheart?"

"Yes, I'm sure I can," she said, although letting go of Brock soaked up most of her remaining courage.

"Stretch up toward me, my lady, and I'll haul you out."

Tentatively Selina pushed away from Brock and held out her hands. She'd jarred her shoulder in the crash and her arms hurt when she shifted, but she suspected she suffered nothing worse than bruising. She was able to move, at least, so she doubted she'd broken any bones. Brock's condition worried her. He'd taken most of the impact of the crash.

The man's hands closed around hers with reassuring firmness. Brock flattened his hands on her rump, ready to push. All this movement inside the cabin made the carriage rock in a most alarming fashion. She bit her lip and told herself that a fit of hysterics would do nobody any good.

"My name is Plaistow," the man said in a calm voice. "Lord Derwent's coachman."

The coincidence of his identity barely registered. She was too frantic to escape the carriage before it overturned.

"Are you ready?" the man asked.

"Yes," she said, sounding surer than she felt.

Between Plaistow pulling and Brock pushing, she managed to climb out of the carriage. Plaistow straightened and held her arm as she found her balance on the road. "Are you all right, my lady?"

She took in the carriage's precarious position, leaning over the deep ditch. It wouldn't take much for the vehicle to overturn completely.

"Yes," she said faintly. Her legs seemed just about capable of holding her up and while her escape from the vehicle had unleashed a volley of aches and pains, she was in one piece. Her dress was torn along one sleeve, and her hair had come down in the accident. But thanks to Brock's heroism, she'd emerged unscathed from what could have been a disaster. "Let me help you with his lordship."

She heard an ominous creak, but when she saw Brock's head emerge from the open doorway, she released a gasp of relief. Although with all that blood smearing his face, he looked ghastly. "Help his lordship, Plaistow."

"Can you stand?"

"Yes." Another creak from the wrecked carriage had her panicking. "Quick, before the coach goes."

Plaistow rushed forward to grab Brock's arms and heave him free. The violent movement was too much for the carriage's equilibrium. With a volley of sharp snaps, the once-opulent vehicle lurched into the ditch, landing with a resounding crash and the tinkle of more broken glass.

Selina rushed up to support Brock before he collapsed to the ground. She staggered as his full weight rested on her.

"All set, my lord?" Plaistow asked. "We were lucky nobody was killed. I thought my time was up, I don't mind telling you."

"Thank you for your help," Brock said, managing to stand on his own feet before she folded under him, thank goodness.

Now the immediate danger passed, Selina started to shake like a leaf. She clung to Brock's arm and dragged in a shuddering breath to clear the fog from her head. For the first time since the accident, she paid attention to her surroundings.

They were standing on an empty stretch of road, with flat, lifeless fields extending around them. It was a cold, bleak place to be stranded. Nobody had done anything to round up the horses since Plaistow had unharnessed them from Brock's carriage. Now the frightened animals milled around, snorting and shying and trailing broken leather straps. It was a miracle that they seemed to have survived the smash without serious harm.

Brock's carriage was beyond repair, so she hoped Plaistow and his passengers were willing to take her and her lover up with them. At the Blue Wagon, Kitty and John would be worried sick about her.

On the edge of the road, Erskine slumped on the ground, nursing his arm. Beyond him, two well-dressed men stood in conversation in the shadow of the other carriage, which appeared to have suffered no damage.

Horror filled her when she realized that one of the men was Lord Derwent. But that was nothing compared to her reaction when the other man turned toward her.

Across the distance, she found herself staring into Cecil Canley-Smythe's appalled face. He made an uncertain step in her direction. "Selina?"

Then he took in the fact that she stood beside one of the most notorious rakes in England, and his features tautened with fury.

CHAPTER ELEVEN

*B*rock felt Selina stiffen beside him, then he heard someone speak her name. He turned from contemplating his wrecked carriage in time for Selina's fiancé to shove him away from her.

Taken by surprise, he didn't offer immediate resistance as Cecil grabbed her arm and wrenched her toward him. "What the devil are you doing here?"

Brock watched the confidence he loved blanch out of her face, leaving her looking ashamed and frightened. "Cecil, I..."

"Let her go," Brock growled.

Cecil sent him a haughty look. "You have no rights over this woman."

"Cecil, please don't make a scene," Selina pleaded, straining back to try and break his hold.

"Canley-Smythe, what is this to-do?" Lord Derwent strode over to Cecil, then he took in Selina and Brock's presence. Aristocratic displeasure hardened his features as he realized who had occupied the other coach. "Mrs. Martin, your servant. Bruard."

"Derwent," Brock said coldly. He struggled to come up with some unexceptional reason for him to be with Selina. "Mrs. Martin has been staying with a friend in the locality, and I arranged to collect her on my way back from my hunting box on the coast."

"I...see," Derwent said slowly. To his chagrin, Brock knew that he did indeed see. Far too much, blast him.

"Mrs. Martin has had a shock, and it's cold out here. Could I prevail upon you to drive her to the Blue Wagon? She has a carriage waiting there to take her to London."

Cecil flung Selina off as if she was infected with some contagious disease. "Better to let the traitorous hellcat freeze."

"Cecil, as Lord Bruard said..." she began, sounding even less convincing than Brock had.

"I didn't come down in the last shower, you lying slut. You've been with that lecherous bastard since I left you."

Brock saw Selina flinch, and he stepped nearer to extend his arm, but she recoiled from his protection. The frozen misery on her face had threatened to break his heart. It was worse now when she refused to accept any help from him.

"Mind your tongue when you speak to the lady," Brock snapped.

"I'll call it as I see it."

Derwent winced. It was clear that he was eager to avoid dramatics. "Canley-Smythe, I realize this encounter is unexpected, but theatrics benefit nobody."

Brock saw Cecil consider a heated response, but self-interest must have kicked in. He wouldn't want to offend such a powerful patron as Lord Derwent. In seething acknowledgment, he bowed.

Derwent nodded, although his expression didn't warm. He presented his arm to Selina. "May I offer you a seat in my carriage, Mrs. Martin?"

"Thank you, but if...if Erskine has a broken arm, he should go. I was only bruised in the accident, my lord."

Pride threatened to burst Brock's chest. Even on what must count as the worst day of her life, she thought of someone else's trouble before her own.

Derwent scowled, as if the idea of a menial sharing the rarefied air he breathed offended every drop of his blue blood. "There's room for four. If we take the injured man, Mr. Canley-Smythe or Lord Bruard must remain behind."

Horror flooded Brock at the prospect of letting Selina go without him. He didn't trust Cecil, who looked ready to commit murder. It was the closest thing to passion he'd ever seen the cod-faced poltroon display. But then Brock had known from the first that while Selina didn't want Cecil, Cecil most definitely wanted her.

Selina broke away to cross to where Erskine sat, pale and in obvious agony. Brock followed, itching to do something to make all this better for Selina and hating to be so powerless.

"We need to splint that arm before you travel, Erskine," she said in an impressively steady voice. "I'm so sorry you were hurt."

"Och, madam, nae need to worry about me. I'll be right as rain in nae time." But when the man tried to stand up, he jarred his arm and went as white as milk.

Relieved to have something practical to do, Brock returned to his carriage. He slithered down the bank and felt his boots sink into the mud as he snapped a length of wood from the rails. He tossed the stick back onto the road, then collected the baggage from the back and tossed that up to safety, too.

Plaistow appeared at the top of the ditch. "May I be of assistance, my lord?"

"Good man. Can you give me a hand up?"

The sides of the ditch were steep and slippery. Brock had made it down with relative ease. He wasn't sure he'd make it out again without help.

When he was back on the road, he rummaged in his bag and produced half a dozen neck cloths. He also took the chance to rub some snow over his face and hands to clean off the worst of the blood.

He turned back to Plaistow. "Will you help me splint my coachman's broken arm?"

By the time Erskine was ready to travel, after an interval of excruciating pain that he bore with impressive stoicism, Derwent and Canley-Smythe had retired inside the undamaged coach. Neither had offered to assist with the coachman's injuries.

"More brandy, Erskine?" Brock asked, as he and Selina helped the stocky young man up onto shaky legs. Now Erskine was as ready to travel as he was going to be, Plaistow had left them to check that his horses were fit to run.

Erskine was ashen, and it was clear shock was setting in. "Aye, thank ye," he mumbled, staggering as he found his feet.

"Keep this." Brock handed the man the silver flask. "You might need it again before you reach the Blue Wagon."

With some stumbling, Brock and Selina got Erskine across to the carriage. Derwent emerged as they approached. "If we take your man, someone has to stay behind."

"Be buggered if I'm giving up my seat for that petticoat-chasing bastard," Cecil snarled from inside the vehicle.

Brock caught a flash of terror in Selina's eyes at the prospect of being trapped with Cecil. He lowered his voice as he spoke to Derwent. "I believe it's best if Mrs. Martin isn't alone with Canley-Smythe."

Derwent still looked as though something in the vicinity stank to high heaven. "You have my word that she'll come to no harm, Bruard."

The sneer he sent Selina indicated that despite his assurances, he believed she deserved all she got. Brock fought back the urge to beat the self-righteousness out of the sod. Right now, he and Selina needed Derwent's help – and his discretion, although Brock had a grim feeling that was too much to ask.

"Thank you," he said, although the words stuck in his craw.

"You can wait here and we'll send back help, or you can follow us on one of your carriage horses," Derwent said coldly.

Now Selina no longer fussed over Erskine, the brief purpose faded from her expression. She was back to looking like the world ended. Damn it all to hell.

"I'll ride one of the horses." He raised his voice so that Cecil heard him and noted that Selina's defender intended to arrive at the inn soon after she did. "I should be just behind you. Derwent, when you get to the Blue Wagon, can you please wait with Mrs. Martin, so that no ruffians annoy her?"

He meant one ruffian in particular. To Brock's relief, Derwent nodded. "It would be my pleasure."

He didn't sound like it would be a pleasure, but at this stage, Brock would take what he could get. "Also could you arrange for someone to return to round up the rest of the horses?"

"Of course."

Brock bowed to Selina and sent her a smile meant to bolster her courage. "Such bad luck that our short trip together ended in grief, Mrs. Martin."

She didn't look up at him. Brock burned to tell her that everything would be fine, that he would make it so. He burned to claim her as his, and consign Cecil to the devil. He burned to take her in his arms and kiss her, until she looked like the brave, vital woman he knew she was at heart, and not this crushed, frightened waif.

But all this burning did him no ounce of good. While they had an audience, he had to do his best to preserve appearances, despite every man here knowing just why Mrs. Martin had shared a carriage with the scandalous Earl of Bruard. Hell, the horses probably knew.

Derwent offered his arm again. "Mrs. Martin, may I assist you inside?"

Selina cast a nervous glance into the shadowy interior. "I think Erskine should go first."

"Erskine, I'll help you," Brock said, before Derwent could protest.

"Thank ye, my lord. I'm gey sorry I'm causing all this palaver."

"I'm sorry you've been injured in my service," Brock said.

Maneuvering a man with a splinted arm into the confined space took more effort and time than either Erskine or Derwent appreciated. Cecil made his displeasure felt when the coachman settled beside him, but Brock was determined that Selina wasn't going to sit next to her betrothed. At least if she sat beside Derwent, she'd have some protection. How Brock loathed that he had to let her go without him, although he'd do his best to catch up before they reached the inn.

Derwent took his seat opposite Cecil and Erskine. Brock caught Selina's arm and spoke under his breath, as she stepped up into the coach. "My darling, I'm hellish sorry…"

"Not now," she muttered and pulled away to find her place. Brock didn't miss the fulminating glare Cecil leveled on her, but he hoped Derwent's presence – and perhaps Erskine's, too – would preserve the niceties as far as the Blue Wagon.

"Shut the damned door," Cecil snarled. "It's bloody freezing."

His heart heavy with guilt, regret and foreboding, Brock slammed the door and stepped back. As the short, cold day closed in toward night, Plaistow set the horses moving.

Selina clasped shaking hands in her lap and told herself that she wouldn't cry. She fixed her gaze on the bleak view out the window, although she didn't see anything of the landscape. Instead, she struggled to come to terms with the mammoth scale of the disaster that had befallen her.

Brock had done his best to place an innocent gloss on her presence, but not even a babe in arms would believe his flimsy story. Nausea churned in her belly when she imagined what might happen now that Cecil had discovered her infidelity.

Not just Cecil. There were other witnesses, apart from a fiancé who, if he had any sense, might see some advantage in smothering the scandal. After a week with the Derwents, she was under no illusion how far the delicious morsel of gossip about prim Mrs. Martin spreading her legs for that libertine Lord Bruard would travel. A morsel made even more delicious, now it included the spicy addition of the lady's betrothed catching her in the seducer's company.

She wanted to sink into the ground and disappear. Shame and fear placed an iron band around her chest, a band that tightened with every second and threatened to cut off her breathing. After the accident, she was sore and stiff, but her physical discomfort didn't come near to matching the rank wretchedness seething in her belly.

Black spots clouded her vision. She realized she was on the verge of fainting – which would lacerate her pride worse than crying. A sharp pain from her lungs reminded her to suck in some air. Her sight cleared, but that offered no relief. Devastation lay in every direction, and she wanted to die of humiliation.

Since Gerald was born, she'd done her best to be a good mother. She'd protected him as far as she could from the effects of his father's excesses. She'd offered him secure and steady love. She'd tried to teach him right from wrong.

Now the almighty scandal about to break over her head would make her son think that his mother was a round-heeled slut. It didn't matter that when Brock touched her, she felt purer than she'd ever felt in her life. She was just another empty-headed strumpet who had succumbed to Lord Bruard's fatal charm. That her stupidity had cost her a marriage to one of the richest men in England provided even greater fodder for tattle. From Land's End to John o'Groats, people would snicker and point their fingers and click their tongues in delighted disapproval.

Selina's hands clenched in her skirts until the knuckles shone white. She didn't know how she could bear the anguish to come.

Even worse, she'd lose her son. Without Cecil, she had no money to support Gerald. Even if she did, his trustees would insist on removing him from her dangerous influence. His grandmother would take him and subject him to the same suffocating treatment that had turned Roderick into a wastrel.

My darling boy, I'm so very sorry.

Selina couldn't imagine that he'd understand. He was too young. And once he left her, the talk would convince him that his mother was a whore. He'd grow up to hate her.

God forgive her, how on earth could she have done this terrible thing?

A cry of distress rose in her throat. Struggling to maintain a dignified silence, she fisted her hands even tighter in her skirts.

The silence in the carriage vibrated with hostility. Poor Erskine looked like he was in terrible pain, and as if he wished he'd stayed behind with Brock's horses. She couldn't blame him. Lord Derwent regarded her as if she was mud beneath his feet. Which was the height of hypocrisy, given that his long-term mistress had been a guest at the recent house party. The highborn ladies might have turned their noses up at Selina, but her presence hadn't restrained their gossiping tongues.

She flinched. Gossiping tongues that would soon flap with tales of the rake, the social-climbing Midas, and the wanton widow.

Cecil sat fuming in the corner. His large body seemed to swell, until it took up more than its share of space. Even unspoken, his rage threatened to blister her skin.

"We're almost at the inn," Derwent said in a distant voice.

Selina should be relieved, but she was sickly aware that once she reached the Blue Wagon, the rest of her life would start. Right now, even the prospect of traveling forever with a livid Cecil and a contemptuous Lord Derwent was preferable to facing up to the unholy mess she'd made of everything.

As she turned away from the window, she made the mistake of catching Cecil's eye. He glared at her as if he hated her. What else did she expect?

But since the accident, curiosity had eaten at her. At last, she dared to ask the question that puzzled her. "Why are you here? I thought you were heading north to see your mill managers."

A sneer twisted his thick lips. "And I thought you were going back to London to prepare for our wedding. It seemed we were both mistaken." His sarcasm turned vicious. "I was indeed mistaken in the virtuous Widow Martin."

She couldn't contain a faint whimper of distress, although more and worse awaited, now her liaison with Brock was sure to become public knowledge.

"I asked Mr. Canley-Smythe to return early from his factories, as I wished to discuss our business at greater length than we managed during the house party," Lord Derwent said.

"A good thing his lordship invited me," Cecil snapped. "Or I'd find myself bound to a woman I'm now ashamed to claim as an acquaintance."

Selina bit her lip and reminded herself that she wouldn't cry in front of Cecil. She wouldn't give him that satisfaction. But it was plaguey difficult to hold onto her composure.

"Nothing to say, Selina?" he jeered.

She could see he was disappointed that she wasn't biting back. But what could she say? He had a right to his temper. She'd betrayed and humiliated him in the worst possible way. And while he might be a bully and a boor, he didn't deserve this.

"Just that I'm sorry, Cecil," she said in a quiet voice, as she linked shaking hands together in her lap. "I have wronged you unforgivably, and there's nothing I can do to make amends."

He went on needling her. "I'll wager you're sorry. You've lost an honorable place as a rich man's wife, in exchange for a few days in a debauchee's filthy bed. You've proven yourself a slut, madam. And a stupid slut to boot."

"Canley-Smythe, that's enough," Derwent snapped, as Selina bit so hard on her lip, she tasted blood.

Cecil's jaw set in an austere line, but he bowed his head to Derwent. "Your pardon, my lord. The strength of my feelings overcame me."

Derwent's tone remained forbidding. "I can understand you're suffering a disappointment, but do me the courtesy of containing yourself while in my company."

"My apologies," Cecil said stiffly, but the scowl he leveled on Selina told her that he had plenty more to say and he intended to find an opportunity say it.

God help her.

At the Blue Wagon, Kitty must have been waiting beside the front door, because she rushed out across the bustling yard in a fluster of relief as soon as Lord Derwent handed Selina from his carriage.

"Miss Selina, thank heaven! I've been that worried about you. I feared some mishap." Kitty's gaze sharpened on her. "Lordy, madam, are you all right? You look terrible."

Selina supposed that "some mishap" could describe the day's calamities. She mustered a smile and struggled to sound as if her life hadn't come to an end. "There was a carriage accident, but I wasn't injured. Just a few bruises. Where is John? I'd like to leave for London straightaway."

The yard was crowded, and there was no sign of Brock. He hadn't passed them on the road, but she'd hoped he wasn't far behind. Luck didn't shine on her today. She was vaguely aware of Cecil climbing out of the carriage. Lord Derwent stood a few feet away, requesting a parlor for his use and ordering assistance for Erskine.

She shrank from the curious glances directed at the new arrivals. Nobody would miss the disheveled woman exiting the stylish equipage in the company of two well-to-do gentlemen and an injured man. She wished she could hide under her bonnet, but she'd left it back in the wrecked carriage.

Selina felt close to shattering. All the emotional turmoil of leaving the hunting box, then the accident, and now this public humiliation – humiliation sure to worsen as the scandal spread – overwhelmed her. She stumbled as she advanced toward the inn's entrance.

"Madam, let me help you." When Kitty placed a supportive arm around Selina's waist, she sagged into her maid's grasp. The girl lowered her voice. "I thought I might see a certain gentleman with you."

Selina spoke under her breath, too. "The earl is following on horseback."

The inn's servants were already bustling around them. Yet more people to bear witness to her disgrace, she thought bitterly. She heard Erskine's strangled groan, as they attempted to move him.

"You and I are due a discussion before you go," Cecil said behind her, in a tone that made the hairs rise on the back of her neck.

"Cecil, tempers are running too high right now." She struggled to sound in control. A concerned glance from Kitty hinted that she didn't succeed. While she owed Cecil an explanation, she didn't want to talk to him while anger rolled off him in waves. "Better you come and see me in London."

The hand that curled around her arm wasn't half so gentle as Kitty's. "No, we should sort this out now, Mrs. Martin."

Since she'd agreed to marry him, Cecil had called her Selina. Her change of status in his life was clear. A harrowing future loomed ahead, but she couldn't contain a surge of relief as she realized that she no longer had to share Cecil Canley-Smythe's bed. Ever since she'd accepted that marrying him was the only way to keep Gerald, the prospect of Cecil's hands on her had made her queasy.

Cecil's grasp was rough on her arm, bruised in the accident, but she refused to quail under his bullying. She straightened away from Kitty and lifted her chin. While she might feel bilious with shame, she refused to cringe as Cecil wanted her to. As they entered the crowded inn, her maid dogged her footsteps.

"This way, sir, madam," the plump landlord said, gesturing down a black-and-white tiled hallway.

Cecil ignored the man and hauled Selina toward the steps. She stiffened and tried to break free. "I'd prefer to remain downstairs," she said, through stiff lips.

Cecil's disdainful glance made her shrink away. "Your wishes no longer carry weight with me, Mrs. Martin."

"Nonetheless, I..."

"Sir, Lord Derwent has requested a private parlor on the ground floor for the lady," the landlord said in a quavering voice. Selina didn't blame him for sounding nervous.

"His lordship has no authority over this female," Cecil snapped.

Selina hid a wince at her demotion from lady to mere female. "Cecil, anything you want to say to me, you can say downstairs."

He lowered his voice, until only she could hear him. "I assume you'd prefer to avoid a scene."

"Surely you would, too," she hissed back. "Any scandal will hurt you as well as me."

The cruel smile that curved his mouth shot another jolt of terror through her. This wasn't a Cecil she'd ever seen. He'd always been overbearing, but now she feared violence. "After the way you've played me for a fool, I could do what I like to you, and no man jack here would raise a finger to stop me."

Selina had a horrid feeling he was right. She was the guilty party. In fact, if Cecil gave her a good beating, most men in the world would cheer him on. In desperation, she twisted to see behind him, praying that Brock might stride into view. But no lean, dangerous man prowled through the doors.

She battled to maintain her composure. "You want to hurt me, I understand that."

"Yes, I do, but you're not worth the effort. I mightn't be born a gentleman, but that doesn't mean I lack standards."

She'd find his reassurance more convincing if at the same time, his hand wasn't crushing the soft flesh of her upper arm. And if he wasn't quivering with barely restrained rage.

"I'll stay with you, Miss Selina," Kitty said staunchly from behind them.

Selina summoned a smile for her. "Thank you, Kitty."

"I've reserved a parlor where Mrs. Martin may wait in private," Lord Derwent said, coming through the door and walking toward them.

"I'd like to stay with his lordship," Selina stammered.

"Touting for a new lover already?"

She flinched at Cecil's spiteful question, but before she could muster a reply, he turned to Derwent. "Mrs. Martin and I have private issues to discuss, my lord. You may rely on my honor."

"I hope so," Derwent said shortly, but despite his promise to Brock, it was clear he wasn't interested in any further attempt to save her skin.

Again Selina craned her neck to catch a glimpse of the door. No Brock. Her stomach scrunched up into a ball of sour fear. Her head pounded with alarm, but she mounted the first step with as much dignity as she could muster.

"Stay close, Kitty," she muttered, as Cecil climbed the stairs ahead of her at a pace that made her stumble in his wake.

Cecil tugged her along a corridor. Selina started to feel dizzy with terror.

"Madam, I think we should go back," Kitty stammered behind her.

Selina did, too. She dug her heels into the wooden floor. "I'll go no further."

"You'll go as far as I say you will," he snarled.

He stopped outside a door and without releasing her, he unlocked it and slammed it open. Selina took a moment to register that this time round, Lord Derwent hadn't invited Cecil to stay at his house. "Get inside, you faithless bitch."

"Sir!" Kitty protested as Cecil shoved a stumbling Selina into a large parlor crammed with ornate, old-fashioned furniture.

He released Selina to whirl around and bundle a squealing Kitty back into the hall. "I've had quite enough of you, you meddlesome jade."

"Sir! Miss Selina!"

Even as Kitty rushed forward to force her way back into the room, he kicked the door shut and locked it. Kitty's shrieks of outrage were now muffled behind several inches of good English oak.

Panic turned Selina's stomach to water, but she knew that if she showed the slightest sign of weakness, Cecil would destroy her. So she raised her chin and regarded him with the pride she'd learned over the last week. "Say your piece, Cecil, then let me go. Gerald is coming home from school tomorrow, and I'd like to be there when he arrives."

Her calm challenge startled Cecil. Given her spineless compliance the last time they'd been together, she couldn't blame him. "You're not fit to be a mother. To think I introduced a trollop like you to my mamma. I blush at the thought. She warned me about you."

"She warned you about me because she was jealous," Selina dared to say. "She wants to be the only woman in your life."

Cecil reddened with anger, and his beefy fists closed at his sides. "You presume to criticize a woman of such spotless reputation? I can't believe I was so deceived in you."

Selina sighed. She had a feeling Cecil's histrionics were likely to continue for a while.

However vile the consequences of becoming a fallen woman, her disgrace offered a new freedom. "I know you want to shout and call me names until Twelfth Night, but let's take it as read. I've deceived and disappointed you, and now there's going to be an almighty scandal when the world will label me a whore and you a dupe. But for the love of God, at least let us part with a modicum of civility."

"Have you no shame?" Astonishment had him gaping at her. "You sound as if you don't give a fig about what's happened."

She didn't give a fig about Cecil, but not even her despairing recklessness let her say that. "Of course I care. I care that I've stained my good name. I care about the scandal. I care that I'm sure to lose Gerald."

"And you care that you've been found out," he said in a snide tone. "I'm assuming that you intended to rush from Bruard's bed to mine and never confess your sins."

She had, at first. And because of that, she supposed she deserved whatever punishment the world meted out. But now she wondered if, even with Gerald's future at stake, she could have steeled herself to accept Cecil as a husband. After experiencing Brock's passion, how could she lower herself to marry Cecil?

She slid the diamond ring from her finger – she'd removed it a week ago, but replaced it this morning before she left the hunting box – and held it out. "Please take this back, Cecil."

He snatched it, which brought him too close for comfort. "I'll find a woman worthy of this ring."

"I hope you do," Selina said, struggling for calm as she watched him shove the ring in his pocket. "Now I'm going downstairs to find my maid and my coachman and set off for London. I can't imagine we'll have reason to meet again. I know you won't believe me, but I bear you no ill will."

His hard stare was somehow more threatening than his earlier blustering. "I suppose you're hoping

Bruard will keep you in luxury. Well, he might for a week or two. But everyone knows his short attention span, when it comes to his tarts."

"I have no idea what Lord Bruard intends," she said coldly.

"I know he's stolen what belongs to me," he snarled.

This time the tide of fear that rushed through Selina turned her blood to ice. *Don't show him you're afraid. Don't show him you're afraid.* She battled to hold onto some authority. "You can't mean to assault me here, Cecil. There's an inn full of people around us to come to my aid."

He grabbed her wrist in a bruising grip and jerked her nearer. "Be damned if I want to marry you anymore."

"I know that," she said through tight lips.

"But that doesn't stop you giving me what you gave that bastard Bruard."

Vomit rose in her throat, and she strained away from him. "Don't be disgusting."

Fury flared in his eyes, and he gripped her wrist so hard that she heard the bones click. "Disgusting, am I?"

She struggled to break free. "Let me go."

"Not until you hear me out, damn you." He paused on an audible inhalation. She saw him fight for control. When he continued, the rage had receded from his eyes, but the lust that replaced it was no improvement. "While marriage is out of the question, everything doesn't have to end between us. If you stooped to play Bruard's mistress, why not be mine? I'll put you up in a discreet house, give you the deeds if you like. Fine clothes. A carriage. A box at the opera. Carte blanche. I'll keep you in luxury, Selina. No more money worries."

"What about Gerald?" she asked bitterly.

Cecil shrugged, as if her son was of no importance. She realized with a sick feeling that her son had never mattered to the man who had almost become his stepfather. "After this, his mother's name will be dragged through the dirt. If you think Derwent will keep quiet about Bruard rogering you, you're more of a fool than I take you for. You've lost any chance of a decent match, my girl. Better me than selling yourself on the streets."

Dear God, what a repugnant picture Cecil painted. "It's not that bad," she said, still struggling to break free.

Cecil sneered. "It is that bad. You're fair game for any man. If you imagine you might find work, ask yourself who in their right mind would employ Bruard's cast-off mistress? The question is will you accept me as your keeper and profit from your offenses – or will you battle on in poverty until you end up swiving anyone who can put food in your belly?"

As her reeling brain winnowed his odious proposition, Selina's heart turned to stone. Cecil was right about so much. She had a nauseating feeling he was right about everything.

"I won't starve." She heard failing courage in her voice. If she accepted Cecil's offer, she could put some money aside and use that to build a new life when she left him. A new identity. Emigrate even.

He must have sensed her wavering, because his vicious grip softened a tad. "Say yes, Selina. You know I want you."

"But I don't want you," she said dully.

She gave a sharp cry of pain when his grip flexed. "You'll find that hanging out for what you want is a luxury you can no longer afford."

She stared up at Cecil. Agony made spots swim in front of her eyes. "Stop it. The answer is no. A hundred times no."

How could she go from Brock's arms to Cecil's? Even the prospect of penury couldn't make her accept this cruel swine as her keeper. And while he spoke as if he rescued her from disaster, his aim was revenge. If she said yes to Cecil's opportunistic offer, he'd bully her without surcease – and she'd have no recourse against him. She was also wise enough to understand that he'd never forgive the blow she'd struck when she took Brock as her lover. Cecil would make her pay over and over. In pain and humiliation and misery.

Her dread of what was to come was like a massive avalanche threatening to crush her. But she wasn't defeated yet. At least not so defeated that she'd crawl into Cecil's bed.

She watched his face change. Blood suffused his cheeks, and his bones hardened until they presented a terrifying mask.

"Your pride is an expensive indulgence," he bit out. "You'll be sorry you rejected me."

"Never," she said, straining back.

"Then you owe me this, you lying bitch."

"Cecil, no!" Selina cried, as he wrenched her higher and whipped his arm around her waist. He released her wrist to grab her hair, pulling it until tears sprang to her eyes.

His mouth, wet and hot and greedy, crashed down on hers. She felt an instant's relief when he let her hair go. But then he captured her chin in a rough hand. As he tugged until she opened her lips, she struggled to close her teeth against a tongue that felt like a slug in her mouth.

Selina fought, but his hold on her head was unbreakable. She lost the ability to breathe. The world darkened to gray fog. Her head filled with an urgent pounding.

On one last despairing surge of energy, she pushed her arm up from where it was trapped between their bodies. With savage force, she raked her nails down his cheek.

Juddering, he wrenched back. "You little harlot. How dare you?"

He clouted her across the face. Pain exploded through her skull. As she staggered to keep her feet, her vision went black.

Amidst the thunder in her head, she thought she heard the crack of breaking wood. Then through her dizziness, she heard Brock. "You fucking bastard!"

Dazed, she shook her head and sucked in a deep breath. When her sight cleared, she realized that she hadn't imagined Brock's arrival.

He was standing over a cowering Cecil. Behind him, the door hung half off its hinges. "I should bloody well kill you. You'd be no loss to the world, you sniveling coward. How dare you raise your fist to a woman?"

An arm slid around her waist, saving her from falling. "I'm here, Miss Selina," Kitty said.

"Don't hit me again," Cecil sobbed. Blood poured from his nose, and Selina discerned no trace of the hulking beast who had attacked her. When she noted the long furrows her nails had made in his cheek, she felt a primitive surge of triumph.

"Don't kill him, Brock," she said in a thick voice. Her shaking hand touched her jaw, as she wondered if Cecil had broken it. Her face felt like it was on fire. "We've got enough trouble already."

CHAPTER TWELVE

B rock sucked in a shuddering breath and struggled to banish the red, killing mist in front of his eyes. When he'd seen Canley-Smythe hit Selina, he'd gladly have run the mongrel through. Only her choked request stopped him from beating the sod to a pulp.

The thought of what might have happened if he'd turned up even ten minutes later made him feel sick to the stomach. Damn it, it had taken him far too long to reach the Blue Wagon. The horse he'd caught and mounted turned out to be unused to a rider on its back, and the makeshift bridle he'd rigged from the harness hadn't helped. He'd wasted too many precious minutes convincing the brute who was master.

Now he hauled an unresisting Cecil up to slam him against the wall. "If I don't kill you, it's because Selina asked me to show mercy. Remember that when you scuttle away into the dark like the cockroach you are."

Cecil whimpered and shrank back. His nose kept bleeding, staining his face and shirt bright red. "I had every right... Oof."

Brock drew his hand back, shaking it to ease the sting in his knuckles. "Want more?"

"No, devil take you. And devil take that shameless jade. You're welcome to the bitch."

Another blow to Cecil's solar plexus had him blubbering and gasping. "All right. All right."

"Apologize to Mrs. Martin."

Despite his physical misery, Cecil was still angry enough for defiance. "I bloody well will not."

"Brock, don't push it," Selina said.

He glanced back at her. She leaned against Kitty, her cheek marred by the red mark Cecil's fist had left. Brock's fury, barely controlled, revived, and he loomed over Cecil. "Apologize, curse you, or I'll kill you where you stand."

Cecil wiped one fat, trembling hand through the gore on his face before he spoke in a constricted mumble. "I'm sorry, Selina. I shouldn't have hit you."

"And?"

Brock started when a hand curled around his tense arm.

"Let him go. He doesn't matter. I don't need his apologies. I just want him out of my sight."

Brock turned to stare down into her face. "As you wish, my darling," he said, noting out of the corner of his eye how the endearment made Cecil bristle.

The man had the sense to stay silent. Good thing, too. Brock was angry enough to tear him limb from limb. Angry and guilty. He should never have left Selina in the man's company. He should have driven the bloody carriage himself, if there was no room inside.

"Thank you," she murmured.

She made to pull away, but Brock caught her hand and kept her at his side as he faced Canley-

Smythe. "You will leave this inn tonight. You will never again approach Mrs. Martin or her son. You will say nothing to her detriment. If I hear a whisper that you've sullied her name by so much as a wink, I will hunt you down and shoot you like the dog you are. Do you understand?"

He saw Cecil wanted to object, but a quick glance at Brock seemed to convince him that discretion was the wiser choice. It certainly was. Brock wasn't in the habit of making idle threats, and he'd welcome the chance to rid the world of this monster.

"I understand," he said sullenly.

"And do you agree?"

A longer pause made Brock's muscles tense in readiness. But in the end, Cecil gave her a brief bow. The unconcealed contempt in the action made Brock itch to hit him again. "I agree. God damn you both to hell."

Brock heard Selina's soft gasp of relief, and her grip on his hand tightened. "Brock, it's over."

Brock released a long hiss, and he felt his shoulders lower. He drew Selina toward the door. "Come, Kitty, your mistress needs you."

"Yes, sir, my lord," the maid said, scurrying to follow them out. Brock's last glimpse of Cecil was of the man slumped against the wall in an attitude of defeat.

"I'm glad you didn't kill him," Selina murmured.

"It's thanks to you that he's alive," Brock snapped.

Now they were out in the corridor, he noticed that a small crowd had gathered in response to the fracas. He put on his most lordly air and glared at them all. A few had already retreated into their rooms before he spoke in the authoritative tone he'd inherited from generations of Highland chieftains. "Just some small trouble. It's sorted out now. Nothing to worry about. The landlord will be informed."

Nobody saw fit to argue and soon their audience had dissipated. Which didn't mean they wouldn't talk about what they'd seen, plague take them.

Once they were alone, Brock stopped to check Selina's injury. Apart from the bruise spreading across her cheek, she was ghostly pale. She looked sad and frightened and unhappy. His heart contorted in agony. He loathed seeing her like this.

"How is your poor face?" With gentle fingers, he turned her cheek up to the lamplight.

He saw her hide a flinch. "I'll live."

Brock struggled to summon an encouraging smile. "Yes, you will, but for the next little while, you'll live with a lovely purple face." His smile vanished, as the true horror of what Cecil had tried to do to her overcame him. "My love, I'm so sorry everything has gone to hell. The last thing I wanted was to cause you harm, and I've gone ahead and spoiled everything. Can you forgive me?"

"Of course I can forgive you. You just saved me." Only when she cast a warning glance behind her did he recall that Kitty shadowed them.

He was too used to having Selina to himself. All of a sudden, the need to hold her in his arms was too strong, Kitty or no Kitty. "Come here. You look like you're about to collapse where you stand."

Brock swung her high against his chest. She made a muffled sound of shock, but to his relief, she curled against him and hooked her hand behind his neck.

He checked back to catch Kitty observing them with unconcealed approval. He approved of the girl, too. If she hadn't waited in the inn yard to catch him the moment he arrived on that half-trained nag, God knew what might have occurred. "Go and see if the landlord can give you some ice for your mistress's face, Kitty. I'll take her to her rooms. They're at the end of the corridor. You might also need to tell the fellow that I'll cover the damage that I did to the door when I broke in."

"Don't you mean we're going to your rooms?" Selina murmured, after Kitty curtsied and hurried away.

"Right now, it's my suite. I reserved it last week. But I'll go downstairs later and tell the landlord it's now yours. I'll organize a separate chamber for myself. It's too late to prevent a scandal, but I'll do what I can to preserve appearances. It's best you stay here tonight. I know you're desperate to get to London, but it's dark outside and you're in no fit state to travel."

"I was so frightened when Cecil attacked me," she confessed in a broken voice, pressing closer.

"He won't frighten you ever again. You should never have left my side." *You should never leave my side.*

"Oh, Brock," she said in a broken voice. She buried her face in his chest and burst into a storm of tears.

His gut twisted into tangled knots as he cuddled her closer. He hated to hear her cry.

"Selina, sweetheart, don't take on so." When he strode down the hallway, his arms tightened around her. "Hush. Hush, my love. He's not worth it."

Brock shouldered his way into the suite's parlor and gently settled her in a chair in front of the blazing fire. He dropped to his haunches before her and fumbled in his coat so he could pass her his handkerchief. "Please stop crying, Selina. It's all right. It's all going to be all right. He was never worthy of you."

"I'm not crying over Cecil," she said thickly, wiping at her eyes. "In fact, one of the few good things about this shambles is that I no longer have to marry that poisonous bully."

"He's an odious toad," Brock said, starting to rise, but pausing when she caught his hand.

"Don't go."

"Some brandy might make you feel better."

"You make me feel better."

A shaken sigh escaped him. The sight of Selina staggering under that blow had taken ten years off his life. It would haunt him forever. "My darling, what am I going to do with you?"

He leaned in and kissed her with great care, because he was agonizingly aware of how hurt she was. Her lips trembled under his. They tasted of tears.

"Cecil *is* an odious toad," she said, with an attempt at a smile. "It's almost worth losing my reputation if it means that I've avoided marrying him."

This time, she let Brock go and pour some brandy. He went down on his knees in front of her and helped her hold the glass steady so she could drink. "Shall I send for a doctor? I imagine a quack is already downstairs, seeing to Erskine."

"No, thank you. I don't want the doctor." She took a few sips before she pushed the glass away. "I've still got all my teeth and while Cecil's fist hurt like blazes, I'm sure I'll heal, even if I look like a fright for a while."

"You could never look like a fright to me." His eyes roved her ashen face. Her lovely hair fell in a knotted tangle. Her eyes were swollen after her tears, and her bruises made him wish he had killed Cecil after all. He emptied the brandy glass – his nerves weren't entirely calm either – and set it on the floor beside him. "Although right now, you do look like you've had a few adventures."

"The world will view me as an adventuress, once word gets out about my affair with the wicked Lord Bruard." The brandy went some way toward restoring her spirits, he was relieved to see. "Adventuresses have adventures."

"Will you mind so much?"

"I don't mind losing Cecil. I mind how all this will affect Gerald."

There was a soft knock on the door. Brock crossed to find Kitty outside, holding a linen bag full of ice. "Thank you, Kitty. Can you please go downstairs and help with my injured coachman, and also talk to the landlord about rooms for you and Mrs. Martin's driver? Use my name."

"Yes, my lord."

He shut the door and carried the ice across to Selina. "Put this on your face. It will help with the bruising."

With unsteady hands, she accepted the bag and pressed it against her jaw. "Thank you."

"Do you feel dizzy? Do you want to lie down?"

Her free hand dismissed his concern. "No. To both questions."

"Do you want more brandy?" He loathed feeling so helpless.

"Stop fussing, Brock. I'm not at death's door." The wry fondness in her tone eased the roiling turmoil in his gut. "Come and sit beside me."

As he had so often at the house in the marshes, he folded himself on the rug at her feet. He caught her hand and brought her fingers to his lips for a kiss.

Quiet reigned long enough to allow the churning rage in his gut to ebb. As so often before, Selina's presence gave him peace. Now word was out about their affair, they faced a hell of a dilemma, but at least they remained together. After a day when he thought he was sure to lose her forever, having her beside him gave him cause for hope.

After a long while, he rose and leaned over her. "How are you feeling?"

Her lips turned down in a smile that looked more convincing. "Like I ran into Cecil's fist."

He didn't smile back. "Do you want more ice?"

She shook her head and passed the dripping bag to him. "No."

The bruise darkened already. Brock stifled a renewed surge of hatred for Cecil, as he crossed to the washstand and dropped the bag in the bowl. Selina's former suitor was lucky he'd made it out of that room alive.

Brock turned to face her. "Shall I ring for dinner? You must be hungry."

She shook her head. "Perhaps later." She paused, and her expression intensified. "Brock, we need to talk."

"No, we don't. We can talk tomorrow, when you're feeling better."

Selina linked her hands in her lap with a nervous gesture he'd first noticed at Derwent Hall. "I...I'd like to talk now. Please."

He would have argued further, if not for that final fervent "please." Hunkering down in front of her, he took her hands. He noticed they were shaking. Delayed reaction to Cecil's attack, or fear about what she meant to say to him?

"What is it, my love?"

Searching brown eyes settled on him. "What happened today has changed everything."

"Aye," he said with a hint of wariness, not sure where she went with this.

A tremulous smile curved her lips, and her next words emerged in a rush. "Now I'm no longer the respectable Widow Martin, I'm free to become a rake's mistress. That is if the rake will have me."

Shock shuddered through him, and he sat back on his heels. "Selina..."

She frowned and spoke even faster, as if afraid he mightn't hang about long enough to hear her out. "You said...you said in the carriage that you want me to stay with you."

"Of course I want you to stay with me," he said with fond impatience, tightening his grip on her hands as she started to pull away.

She raised her chin. "Then I will stay with you."

He released her and rose, a wry smile twisting his lips. "I'm devilish happy to hear that."

Her frown deepened. "You don't sound happy."

His hand swept through the air. "You weren't born to be someone's mistress, Selina."

To his horror, hurt darkened her eyes and she pressed back against the chair's floral chintz upholstery. "Have today's events convinced you that I'm too much trouble?"

Brock shook his head. "Never. Anyway, the blame for this mess is all mine."

She didn't look convinced. "No, it's my fault. I'm the one who ignored the dictates of morality. I set out to deceive Cecil. Losing Gerald is a fair punishment for what I've done. I'm not a fit mother."

Brock stared at her aghast. "By God, tell me you don't mean that."

"I don't." She made a despairing gesture. "Although I ought to. After today, the world will call me every vile name under the sun."

He released a sigh of relief. "You sounded as if you hated yourself."

Her expression didn't ease. "I might in the future." She spoke with renewed determination. "But first, for as long as you'll have me, I intend to go well and truly to the bad in your company."

He should be overjoyed that she consented to stay with him, but his heart cramped with pity as he looked at her, so brave, so ardent, so fragile. "You ask so little of life. You humble me."

"If you give me more of what we shared at the hunting lodge, that's more than a little."

"No," he said slowly. "No, it's not enough."

"You're frightening me, Brock." She stared up at him with an anxious expression. "Have I got it wrong? Don't you want me anymore?" Her voice cracked on the last word.

He fought the urge to catch her up in his arms and carry her through to the next room, where a large bed waited in the shadows. The communication between their bodies was always perfect.

He spread his hands. "I'll die wanting you, Selina."

His declaration didn't seem to reassure her. "Then why are you hesitating?"

Brock straightened and squared his shoulders. This week had been the most important part of his life. These next few minutes were the most important part of that week. "I don't want you as my mistress, Selina, although I'll always cherish knowing that you offered to come to me without any promises."

To his horror, he watched the blood drain from her face. The bruise stood out starker than ever. She bit back a whimper of distress. "I...I see."

He hissed with self-disgust and ran his hand through his hair. "Hell, I'm making a complete dog's dinner of this. Forgive me."

Her chin rose with a bravado that became tattered with overuse. "It's not easy to give a mistress her marching orders."

Despite the fraught atmosphere, a grunt of bleak laughter escaped him. "I've never found that the case." He stepped forward and caught her hands again, drawing her to her feet with gentle insistence. "I'm not giving you your marching orders, you muddleheaded lassie. Nor am I asking you to be my mistress."

She tried to withdraw, but he held firm. The gaze that always pierced to his soul examined his face. "I don't understand."

He gathered all his courage. Odd how terrifying this was. At this moment, he was more afraid than he could ever remember feeling. Perhaps because nothing in his selfish, ramshackle, hedonistic life had ever meant so much. "Selina, can't you see that I'm trying to work my way up to a proposal?"

"A proposal?" she repeated, as if the word made no sense.

"Will you marry me, sweetheart?"

He waited for some joyful reaction, because he was sure that after the week they'd just spent together, she must feel as he did. Instead moisture filled beautiful eyes that, in his opinion, had already shed enough tears for the day. "Oh, Brock, you're too good."

He frowned with bewilderment and the beginnings of hurt. This wasn't the response he'd expected.

"That's not something I've ever heard anyone say about me," he said dryly, even as uncertainty stirred inside him like a snake in a woodpile.

Uncertainty was an unfamiliar companion, and he could already tell he didn't like it.

A shaky smile curved her soft lips. "Well, you should have. The awful thing is if I had no principles, I'd leap to accept your offer and rush you off to the altar this very minute."

"Feel free," he said, meaning it.

She released one of his hands to wipe her overflowing eyes. "You know, I'm not sure a fallen woman can afford principles."

"What are you trying to say?"

Her throat moved as she swallowed. "You're attempting to rescue me from the price of my folly."

"I'm not trying to rescue you, Selina," he said with some heat.

"Yes, you are. And I honor you for it." She broke away and backed toward the fire. "You're an earl, Brock. I'm an impecunious widow of no particular distinction. Even before I lost my reputation and we set off what promises to be an almighty brouhaha, you could look much higher than an obscure doctor's daughter for a bride."

The gallant, great-hearted fool. She was trying to shield him from the consequences of misguided chivalry. When they both knew that her only hope for restoring her good name and keeping her son was to wed the man who had ruined her.

"I could look no higher than you, Selina."

Her smile threatened to shatter his heart, it was so utterly without hope. "I'll treasure hearing you say that, Brock. But I'll manage."

He stepped forward and seized her hands again. "Don't you want more from life than just managing?"

Wide eyes studied his face. "I don't want another marriage without love."

"Is that what ours would be?"

She looked confused. "Well, you know that I love you. I haven't tried to hide it, and you're so experienced with women, you can't have missed it."

She'd given him so much joy over this last week, yet of all the gifts she'd granted him, this was the greatest. "I'd hoped."

She looked startled. "Did you?"

"Of course, my darling." His heart raced with excitement. For a few minutes there, he'd feared that she meant to reject him. He never wanted to feel like that again. "You see, it's always so much better if, when a fellow loves a woman as much as I love you, the woman in question loves him back."

Brock watched her expression change. Such happiness illuminated her features that he was dazzled. But the elation only lasted a moment before doubt darkened her eyes once more. "You're not just saying this because we're in the most awful fix?"

"My darling, let me convince you." He swept her into his arms for a passionate kiss. He'd expected her to hesitate, but she melted into his embrace as though she ached for their sublime connection just as much as he did.

Over these last glorious days, they'd kissed so often. Now he shared his soul with her, as his lips explored hers – gently, because she'd been hurt.

When he returned to the real world, he was in the chair in front of the fire and Selina was draped across his lap with her hands linked behind his neck.

"Do you believe I love you?" he asked, not needing the answer anymore, because every star in the heavens had come down to shine in her eyes.

"Yes, Brock," she said. He had a sudden poignant memory of overhearing her in the Derwents' library. How far they'd come since that night.

He gave her a quick kiss. "And you love me?"

"Oh, yes, so much." A frown drew her fine brows together. "But you still don't have to marry me."

He caught her unbruised cheek in one hand, tilting her face until she met his gaze. "Yes, I do. Do you think I'd allow a dangerous woman like you to wander around unclaimed? I need to take you into my keeping. It's my civic duty."

She gave a husky laugh. "They should give you a medal."

He nodded and spoke in a solemn voice. "They should indeed." He paused. "Anyway, I've wanted to marry you for a long time. It's not just because our misdeeds have been exposed."

"A long time?" The wry smile he loved lengthened her lips. "We've only known each other a week."

"Two actually."

"Well, two."

"In fact, I was in the middle of phrasing my proposal, when we suffered the inconvenience of crashing into a ditch."

"Oh, Brock..." He watched Selina struggle to recall the conversation. So much had happened since, he couldn't blame her for being a little fuzzy on the details.

"I asked you to stay with me."

"You did. I thought..."

"That I was talking about more of what we'd already done."

"But that was so wonderful."

"Yes, it was. But I'd already decided that I want more. I want to sleep beside you every night for the rest of my life. I want to see you grow large as you carry my baby. I want to share life's sorrows and joys with you. I want to see how you change through the years ahead. I want you to go through those changes at my side. In short, I want you as my wife, not my mistress, however exquisite a mistress you make." He frowned. "Now what the devil have I said to make you cry, you lunatic woman?"

With another choked laugh, she wiped her eyes. "If I didn't already love you, Brock, I'd love you after that beautiful speech."

His hold tightened. "Do you love me enough to call me husband? I haven't led a conventional life. I'm a wild and wicked reprobate. I've committed more sins than I could list in a month of Sundays. But through all that, for what it's worth, I've remained a man of my word. I give you my word, Selina, that from now on, you're the only woman in my life. You'll hold my heart forever."

She drew his head down for another kiss that felt like a silent pledge of fealty to match the spoken one he'd just given her. "I love you, Brock," she whispered when they drew apart.

"So does that mean you'll take me on?"

She smiled, and her voice emerged with an immovable certainty that seized hold of his longing heart and opened a vista to the golden future ahead. "I'd be honored, my lord."

EPILOGUE

Bruard Castle, Western Highlands of Scotland, June 1824

Selina stirred from a light doze. She was warm and comfortable – and something seemed to be tickling her nose. She opened heavy-lidded eyes to see that Brock teased her with a buttercup.

"Wake up, sleepyhead," he murmured, discarding the flower. He was stretched out beside her and leaning on one elbow so he could watch her.

"I'm sorry. I must have dropped off."

They were high on a hillside, overlooking the medieval splendors of Bruard Castle in the glen. The summer sun shone down with almost Mediterranean heat, and the remains of a lavish picnic surrounded them.

Below, she could see figures moving around the massive keep as the household readied itself for tonight's visitors. The Laird of Achnasheen, his lady, and their three children were traveling from the coast to spend the next week at Bruard.

As Selina drowsily surveyed the activity, two people in particular captured her attention. Plaistow now worked at Bruard and trained to take over the steward's position when the current man retired at the end of the year. Since his arrival, Plaistow and Kitty had developed an understanding. At this distance, it was hard to tell, but she thought they just might be holding hands.

Brock bent his head toward her, then paused as she gave a great yawn. Followed by the sort of giggle that Roderick Martin's downtrodden wife would never have permitted herself.

Expressive eyebrows arched. "You're dropping off a lot in recent days."

It was true. She was revoltingly somnolent. Most of the time, she found it almost impossible to keep her eyes open. "I'm sorry. It can't be very entertaining for you."

A wicked light entered his dark green eyes, turned them gleaming emerald. "You're entertaining enough when you're awake to make up for any amount of sleeping."

"That's a relief," she murmured and tunneled her hand through his hair, bringing him down for the kiss she'd been so rude to delay.

By the time he raised his head, they were both breathing unsteadily.

"Do you have something to tell me, Selina?" he murmured.

Shocked, she stared up into his striking features. After six months of marriage, his handsomeness still made her heart perform somersaults. "I might have."

One hand slid over her hip to rest on her midriff. "Perhaps news of a happy event?"

Her laugh held a hint of chagrin. "I don't know how I imagined I'd keep it from you. I wanted it to be a surprise."

"It is. A lovely surprise." He leaned over to kiss her stomach. "A son or daughter around Christmas, I think."

He rested his head on her pretty yellow and white muslin skirts, above the place where her body sheltered his child.

Emotion roughened her voice, as she stroked the thick silk of his hair, warmed with the sun. "Yes. That's what Betty says, anyway."

Betty, the estate healer and midwife, had pronounced her as healthy as a horse. Selina had great faith in Betty. Her skills had brought Erskine's broken arm back into full working order.

"How did you know?"

Brock raised his head and sent her a knowing look.

"I'm a silly goose." Selina blushed. "How could you not know?"

"Apart from that, you've developed a new habit of snoring at the drop of a hat and you've been unwell several mornings." He cast a sly glance at the empty picnic basket. "And over recent weeks, you seem to want to eat for England."

She gave an uncomfortable laugh and struggled to sit up. "I fear I'm going to get horribly fat."

He slid his arm around her and drew her into his side. "I rather fancy a plump little pigeon in my bed."

She sighed and rested her head on his shoulder. "There won't be any 'little' about it, I fear." She snuggled closer. "Are you pleased?"

"I'm the happiest man in Scotland, my love."

"I'm glad. I'm pleased, too. Gerald is getting a little too spoiled here in the castle. A baby to divert everyone's attention will do him no harm at all."

"He's happy, my darling. As am I. So very happy. I couldn't have imagined being so happy." He tilted her head up and kissed her with the tenderness that never failed to make her melt. "Thank you."

Settling into his arms, she stared down at the fairytale view below, as her memory sifted through the changes these last rapturous months had wrought. On Christmas Eve, she and Brock had married by special license, and he'd brought her up to Scotland straight afterward. She had no doubt that tongues had wagged about the scandalous start to the Earl of Bruard's marriage. But here in Scotland, London society and its trivial concerns seemed a million miles away. She and Brock established their own kingdom where the only rule was love.

Selina had worried that Gerald might resent Brock the way he'd resented Cecil. But the two males she loved had soon established a strong rapport. When she'd expressed how pleased she was that her misgivings proved unfounded, Brock had laughed. Apparently, Gerald had confessed that he was so relieved to escape Cecil as a stepfather, he'd decided to like Brock from the outset.

Gerald's pleasure in his new life was one of her joys. He had a tutor and a band of rough-and-tumble friends on the estate. When Brock presented him with a horse for his birthday, that only cemented his affection for his new stepfather.

But her greatest joy in her new life was the bond she shared with her husband. He'd never shown any sign of restlessness with their quiet country life, and he looked ten years younger than the cynical rake she'd sighed after at the Derwents' house party last winter.

"You've made my life complete, my bonny wife," Brock said quietly, as though he, too, had been contemplating their time together. "I'd always felt like a boat drifting in a storm. With you, I've reached safe harbor. Now we have a new baby to add to our family. It's almost too much. I love you, Selina."

She tipped her chin until she met his eyes. They glowed with such adoration, she blinked away tears. "And I love you, Brock."

Tender amusement filled his smile. "Over these last weeks, you've also been more inclined to cry."

"I know." She gave a watery giggle. "Isn't it terrible?"

He kissed her again. "It's going to be an interesting six months."

"I hope I'm awake to see them," she said, which made him laugh.

"I can think of something that always wakes you up. We don't have to be back at the castle to get ready for Fergus and Marina for hours yet. May I interest you in some open-air dalliance, my Lady Bruard? I believe there's a convenient summerhouse over the next rise."

Selina brought Brock's head down for a more thorough kiss. "My Lord Bruard, I thought you'd never ask."

ABOUT THE AUTHOR

Australian Anna Campbell has written 11 multi award-winning historical romances for Avon HarperCollins and Grand Central Publishing. As an independently published author, she's released more than 30 bestselling stories. Right now, she is working on a new series called A Scandal in Mayfair, set amidst the glamour and sensuality of Regency London. Anna has won numerous awards for her stories, including RT Book Reviews Reviewers Choice, the Booksellers Best, the Golden Quill (three times), the Heart of Excellence (twice), the Write Touch, the Aspen Gold (twice), and the Australian Romance Readers' favorite historical romance (five times).

Anna loves to hear from her readers. You can find her at:

Website: www.annacampbell.com

facebook.com/AnnaCampbellFans

twitter.comAnnaCampbellOz

bookbub.com/authors/anna-campbell

The Laird's Willful Lass:
The Lairds Most Likely Book 1

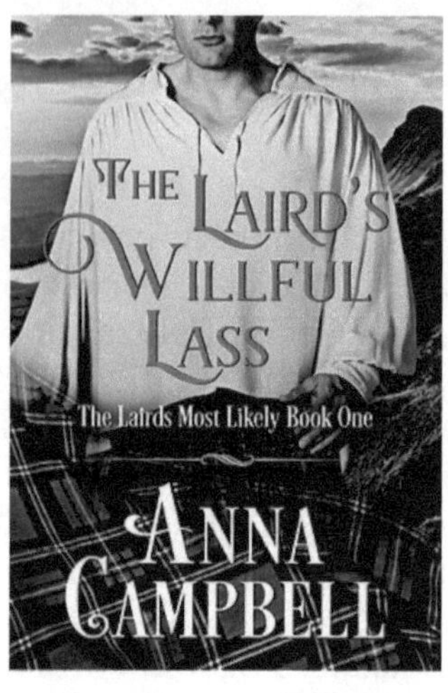

***An untamed man as immovable as a
Highland mountain...***

Fergus Mackinnon, autocratic Laird of Achnasheen,
likes to be in charge. When he was little more than
a lad, he became master of his Scottish estate, and
he's learned to rely on his unfailing judgment. So
has everyone else in his corner of the world. He sees
no reason for his bride—when he finds her—to be
any different.

***A headstrong woman from the warm and
passionate south...***

Marina Lucchetti knows all about fighting her way
through a wall of masculine arrogance. In her
native Florence, she's become a successful artist, no
easy feat for a woman. Now a commission to paint a
series of Highland scenes promises to spread her

fame far and wide. When a carriage accident strands her at Achnasheen for a few weeks, it's a mixed blessing. The magnificent landscape offers everything her artistic soul could desire. If only she can resist the impulse to smash her easel across the laird's obstinate head.

When two fiery souls come together, a conflagration flares.

Marina is Fergus's worst nightmare—a woman who defies a man's guidance. Fergus challenges everything Marina believes about a woman's right to choose her path. No two people could be less suited. But when irresistible passion enters the equation, good sense soon jumps into the loch.

Will the desire between Fergus and Marina blaze hot, then fade to ashes? Or will the imperious laird and his willful lass discover that their differences aren't insurmountable after all, but the spice that will flavor a lifetime of happiness?

The Laird's Christmas Kiss:
The Lairds Most Likely Book 2

Down with love!

Ever since she was fifteen, shy wallflower Elspeth Douglas has pined in vain for the attentions of dashing Brody Girvan, Laird of Invermackie. But the rakish Highlander doesn't even know she's alive. Now she's twenty, she realizes that she'll never be happy until she stops loving her brother's handsome friend. When family and friends gather at Achnasheen Castle for Christmas, she intends to show the world that she's all grown up, and grown out of silly crushes on gorgeous Scotsmen. So take that, my gallant laddie!

Girls just want to have fun...

Except it turns out that Brody isn't singing from the same Christmas carol sheet. Elspeth decides she's not interested in him anymore, just as he decides he's very interested indeed. In fact, now he looks more closely, his friend Hamish's sister is pretty and funny and forthright – and just the lassie to share his Highland estate. Convincing his little wren of his romantic intentions is difficult enough, even before she undergoes a makeover and becomes the belle of Achnasheen. For once in his life, dissolute Brody is burdened with honorable intentions, while the lady he pursues is set on flirtation with no strings attached.

Deck the halls with mistletoe!

With interfering friends and a crate of imported mistletoe thrown into the mix, the stage is set for a house party rife with secrets, clandestine kisses, misunderstandings, heartache, scandal, and love triumphant.

The Highlander's Lost Lady:
The Lairds Most Likely Book 3

A Highlander as brave and strong as a knight of old...

When Diarmid Mactavish, Laird of Invertavey, discovers a mysterious woman washed up on his land after a wild storm, he takes her in and tries to find her family. But even as forbidden dreams of sensual fulfillment torment him, he's convinced that this beautiful lassie isn't what she seems. And if there's one thing Diarmid despises, it's a liar.

A mother willing to do anything to save her daughter...

Widow Fiona Grant has risked everything to break free of her clan and rescue her adolescent daughter from a forced marriage. But before her quest has barely begun, disaster strikes. She escapes her brutish kinsmen, only to be shipwrecked on Mactavish territory where she falls into her enemies' hands. For centuries, a murderous feud has raged between the Mactavishes and the Grants, so how can she trust her darkly handsome host?

Now a twisted Highland road leads to danger and passion...and irresistible love. But is love strong enough to banish the past's long shadows and offer these wary allies all that their hearts desire?

The Highlander's Defiant Captive:
The Lairds Most Likely Book 4

Peace in the glens means war in the bedchamber!

Scotland. 1699. In a time of heroes, the greatest hero of all is Callum Mackinnon, Laird of Achnasheen. Brave, reckless, canny, and handsome enough to turn any lassie weak at the knees, Callum is a legend in the wild corner of the Highlands where he rules. Now the young laird is determined to choose a new path for his clan and end the violent feud with the Drummonds, a conflict that has painted the glens red with blood for centuries. This means taking Bonny Mhairi Drummond, the Rose of Bruard, as his wife. When negotiations with her pig-headed father break down, Callum seizes matters into his own hands and kidnaps the fairest maiden in Scotland, swearing to make her his own.

Bonny Mhairi is the adored only child of Clan

Drummond's doughty chieftain and she's inherited all her father's courage and stubbornness. Not to mention his undying hatred for anyone called Mackinnon. When the Mackinnon chieftain steals her away from her home and vows to woo her into accepting him as her husband, she swears that she'll never consent to be his bride. But trapped inside her foe's castle, Mhairi finds it hard to cling to old certainties. She detests her arrogant jailer, even as he sparks a fierce, forbidden hunger in her soul.

Loving the enemy...

As Callum and Mhairi wage their passionate war of hearts, danger, treachery and desire circle closer and closer. When her father's army masses at the gates of Achnasheen, will Mhairi prove herself a Drummond now and forever? Or will new allegiances trump ancient hatred, as the desperate laird battles to win the lass he loves more than his life?

The Highlander's Christmas Quest:
The Lairds Most Likely Book 5

She's found the man for her, but he has no plans to stay on her island. Perhaps it's time to try a little sabotage!

Scotland. 1725. The moment she sees handsome Dougal Drummond, Kirsty Macbain tumbles headlong into love. A chance storm a few days before Christmas has blown the gallant Highlander off-course to her father's isle of Askaval, but once he's repaired his boat, Dougal is determined to continue on his way. His bright blue eyes are firmly fixed on valiant deeds and a distant horizon. What does he care for a smart-mouthed, independent lassie who forms no part of his plans for his future?

Kirsty is convinced that if only she can keep Dougal on Askaval, he'll see how perfect they are together. With his boat out of action, he's trapped in her company. Some surreptitious midnight destruction with a drill and a hammer might help true love to win out. On the other hand, if Dougal discovers what she's been up to, there will be the devil to pay.

Will this madcap Christmas deliver Kirsty's heart's desire – or will her scheming see Dougal sailing away to a life without her?

The Highlander's English Bride: The Lairds Most Likely Book 6

An impossible pairing...

Hamish Douglas, the mercurial Laird of Glen Lyon, has never got along with independent, smart-mouthed Emily Baylor. Which wouldn't matter if this brilliant Scottish astronomer didn't move in the same scientific circles as Emily and if her famous father wasn't his mentor. But when Emily looks likely to derail the event which will make Hamish's career, he loses his temper with the pretty miss and his recklessness leaves her reputation in ruins.

A marriage made in scandal...

Emily has always thought her father's spectacular protégé was far too arrogant for his own good. But what is she to do when the only way she can save her good name in society is to wed the unruly laird? Reluctantly she accepts Hamish's proposal, but only on the condition that their union remains chaste. That shouldn't be a problem; they've never been friends, let alone potential lovers – except that after they marry, Hamish reveals unexpected depths and a host of admirable qualities, and he's so awfully handsome, and now the swaggering rogue admits that he desires her...

From the ballrooms of London to the grandeur of the western Highlands, a battle royal rages between these two strong-willed combatants. Neither plans to yield an inch – but are these smart people smart enough to see that sometimes the greatest victory lies in mutual surrender?

The Highlander's Forbidden Mistress: The Lairds Most Likely Book 7

A week to be wicked...

Widowed Selina Martin faces another marriage founded on duty, not love. When notorious libertine Lord Bruard invites her to his isolated hunting lodge, he promises discretion – and seven days of hedonistic pleasure before she weds her boorish fiancé. All her life, Selina has done the right thing, but this no-strings-attached chance to discover the handsome rake's sensual secrets is irresistible. She'll surrender to her wicked fantasies, seize some brief happiness, then knuckle down to a loveless union. What could possibly go wrong?

In a lifetime of seduction, Brock Drummond, the dashing Earl of Bruard, has never wanted a woman the way he wants demure widow Selina Martin. When Selina agrees to become his temporary lover, he soon falls captive to an enchantment unlike any other. He sets out to slake his white hot desire until only ashes remain, but as each day of forbidden delight passes, the idea of saying goodbye to his ardent mistress becomes more and more unbearable.

When scandal explodes around them and threatens to destroy Selina, Brock is the only person she can turn to. After so short a time, can she trust a man whose name is a byword for depravity?

Will this sizzling liaison prove a mere affair to remember? Or will their week of passion spark a lifetime of happiness for the widow and her dissolute Scottish earl?

The Highlander's Christmas Countess: The Lairds Most Likely Book 8

The new stableboy has a secret!

Kit Laing is a genius with Glen Lyon's horses and a favorite with his employer's family, but he isn't all he seems. In fact, the shy stablehand isn't a he at all. Kit is actually Christabel Urquhart, Countess of Appin, on the run from a greedy, violent stepbrother with designs on her fortune.

And the laird's handsome nephew has worked out just what it is.

Quentin MacNab, the dashing heir to Cannich, has had his suspicions about the new stable lad from the first. Kit is far too pretty to be a boy – and far too well spoken to be a servant.

Now passion and danger combine to create a Yuletide like no other.

When a snowstorm traps Kit and Quentin overnight in an isolated hut, the discovery of her true identity sparks a rushed marriage to stave off a scandal. But can the Christmas Countess learn to trust her charming new husband's promises of protection? Or will their fragile alliance fall victim to the evil forces assailing her?

The Highlander's Rescued Maiden: The Lairds Most Likely Book 9

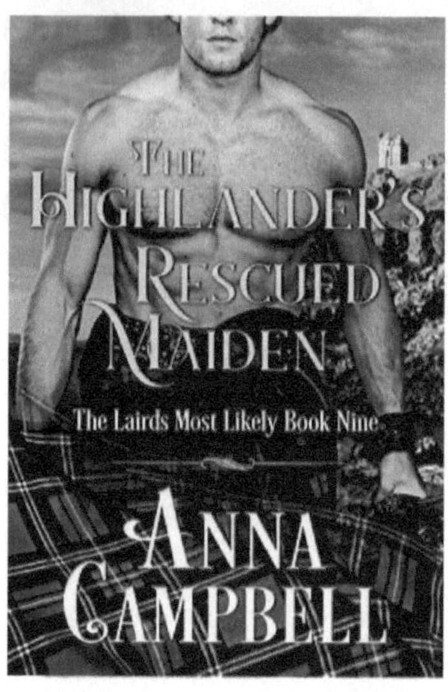

The myth of Fair Ellen of the Isles.

Across the Highlands, people recount the legend of a beautiful lassie in a tower, locked away from her clamorous suitors by a tyrannical father. Any person of sense dismisses the story as a fairy tale, no more substantial than a wisp of Scottish mist.

Rogue or hero? Or a little bit of both?

Dashing Highlander Will Mackinnon is a devil with the ladies, disinclined to fall for such romantic nonsense. But one day, his storm-tossed boat washes ashore at a rocky island dominated by a stone tower. Inside the tower, he discovers lovely, gallant Ellen Cameron and a passion that eclipses anything he's experienced before in his reckless life.

Danger and desire...

This brave adventurer vows to rescue the captive maiden and make her his own forever. But dark shadows gather about the lovers and threaten to destroy all their hopes for happiness. Will has found the love of a lifetime – but will it end up costing him his life?

thought to see again, the man who betrayed her.
When she was pregnant with his son, Malcolm
abandoned her to find her way alone in a cold,
heartless world. Now she discovers that her long-
held hatred is based on lies and that he's been true
to her. Yet surely after all these years, it's too late to
awaken the love that once united them.

*As Christmas Eve turns into Christmas
Day, Malcolm and Rhona discover that
their mutual desire has never died. Will this
Yuletide reunion lead to a lifetime
together? Or has old tragedy ruptured their
bond forever?*

www.ingramcontent.com/pod-product-compliance
Lightning Source LLC
Chambersburg PA
CBHW030751190726

48285CB00003B/806